THE SPIRIT FLYER SERIES

THE ONLY GAME IN TOWN

Win, and You Lose the Best Prize of All

JOHN BIBEE

Illustrated by Paul Turnbaugh

INTERVARSITY PRESS
DOWNERS GROVE, ILLINOIS 60515

InterVarsity Press is the book publishing division of InterVarsity Christian Fellowship, a student movement active on campus at hundreds of universities, colleges and schools of nursing. For information about local and regional activities, write Public Relations Dept., InterVarsity Christian Fellowship, 6400 Schroeder Rd., P.O. Box 7895, Madison, WI 53707-7895.

Cover illustration: Paul Turnbaugh

ISBN 0-8308-1202-2

Printed in the United States of America

Library of Congress Cataloging in Publication Data

Bibee, John.
    The only game in town / by John Bibee; illustrated by Paul
Turnbaugh.
      p. cm.—(The Spirit Flyer series; 3)
    Summary: Daniel, a new boy in Centerville, struggles over whether
to join the evil but tempting Cobra Club or align himself with the
children who ride the Spirit Flyer bicycles.
    ISBN 0-8308-1202-4
    [1. Fantasy.] I. Turnbaugh, Paul, ill. II. Title. III. Series:
Bibee, J. Spirit Flyer series; 3.
PZ7.B471464On 1988
[Fic]—dc19

88-9369
CIP
AC

17 16 15 14 13 12 11 10 9 8 7 6 5 4
99 98 97 96 95 94 93 92

For Lucinda, may our oneness grow . . .

THE BIKE
CAME
BACK
· · · · · · · ·

1

Some things don't add up. Once there was a town where everyone was so busy counting things that they forgot what really counted. . . .

Centerville was a small, friendly town. There were many friendly grownups and friendly children. There were even friendly dogs and cats and a few nice horses. Life was fairly peaceful in Centerville. But things were changing.

Toward the end of the summer, the old factory on the west edge of town opened back up. Goliath Industries were the new owners. People were moving into Centerville—something that hadn't happened for a long time. In fact, so many new people were moving into town that new houses were being built for the first time in twenty years.

The Bayley family was one of the first families to arrive. The big moving truck was parked in front of a house on Oak Street. The Saturday morning was warming up quickly since it was the first week of August, the hottest time of the year in Centerville.

The last box was rolled out of the moving truck. Upstairs in the house, Daniel Bayley was unpacking boxes in his new room when he heard his mother yell out his name. Something about the tone of her voice didn't sound right.

The boy moved with a noticeable limp across his room out into the hallway. Daniel held carefully onto the railing as he went downstairs.

"Hold it right there, young man," Mrs. Bayley said at the bottom of the steps. She put her hands on her hips and blocked his way. Daniel stopped. He looked at his mother's stern face, then looked down at his sneakers. Only his mother, he thought, could make you feel guilty even before you were accused.

"I want to show you something," Mrs. Bayley said.

"Ok," Daniel said curiously. He brushed his hand through his bright red hair. The boy had startling clear green eyes and a face full of freckles.

He followed his mother to the garage. When he saw the old red bicycle, the boy's eyes lit up and a huge smile crossed his face.

"It came!" he cried. He squatted down, running his hands over the metal, checking for damage. The bike, though old, appeared to be ok. Below the handlebars were three golden crowns linked together. And on the middle bar in flowing white letters was the name: *Spirit Flyer*.

Daniel pushed up the kickstand and rolled the big bike back and forth. The Spirit Flyer's big balloon tires rolled easily. Though the bike was something of an antique, it was still in very usable condition. An old cracked mirror was fastened to the handlebars along with a big horn with a rubber bulb, a gearshift lever, a gauge that looked something like a speedometer and a large headlight. A small bottle-shaped generator was attached to the metal frame that held the back tire. He hopped on, then pedaled in a small circle in the driveway. Daniel couldn't stop smiling. He was so happy to see the old bike. You would have thought it was an old friend, which in a way, it was.

He then rolled it back into the garage, parking it next to another bike that was already resting on its kickstand. The other bike couldn't have been more different from the old red bike. It was a new, sleek ten-speed, shining with gold metallic paint and black trim. The wheels were made of some of the strongest yet lightest alloy metal available. All the other metal parts were coated in rich shiny chrome. On the middle bar, written in black letters was the name: *Goliath Super Wings.*

Daniel didn't even seem to notice the new bike. He was still so surprised and happy to see the Spirit Flyer that he just kept smiling. But the smile left his freckled face when he saw his mother. She was standing on the lawn in her high heels talking to the moving men. Even though it was Saturday morning, she wore her high heels and skirt as if she were at work. His mom was always dressed up, he thought. Her black hair was combed into a bun, and she had on her make-up.

His ten-year-old sister, Denise, was standing next to his mom. Denise wore a green dress and good shoes. Daniel was wearing his frazzled old blue jeans, sneakers and a ragged green t-shirt. He knew his mother didn't approve, but he liked his old clothes because they were comfortable.

Mrs. Bayley motioned for Daniel to come over. Denise was smiling. She sensed Daniel was in trouble, and she was enjoying every second of it.

"None of these men packed that bicycle in the truck," Mrs. Bayley said as Daniel walked over. "And neither did Denise, so that leaves you. You deliberately sneaked that old bike on after I told you we would bring it later."

"I didn't pack it," Daniel said truthfully. He looked at his mother's face. He didn't look away or he knew she would think he was lying. Mrs.

Bayley stared at Daniel in silence for a long time. Her mouth was one tight little line. The moving men got into the truck. The big truck roared to life, then rumbled down the street.

"Then I suppose you are going to tell me it packed itself on the truck and rolled into the garage by itself?" Mrs. Bayley said.

"Well, it got here somehow," Daniel replied innocently. "Maybe it just came by itself like when I first got it."

Mrs. Bayley opened her mouth to reply but seemed speechless. She stared at the bicycle uneasily for moment, as if remembering something. Then she frowned at her son.

"Daniel, we are new to this town, and I hoped we would be getting off to a good start," Mrs. Bayley said. "I know it's been hard on you children since the divorce. But you live with me, not your father, and you abide by my rules. I took the job with Goliath to get you kids out of the city and into a small town. But we aren't even unpacked, and you're already causing problems again with that stupid old bicycle. Didn't I get you a perfectly good, brand new Goliath bicycle?"

"I don't want another bicycle," Daniel said softly. But his mother wasn't listening.

"You live in a dream world with that old bike, and I don't like it," Mrs. Bayley said crossly. "It's time you woke up. A little pretending is fine, but you've gone way past that. And now you are lying about it."

"But I'm not lying," Daniel said. "I didn't sneak it in the truck. The Spirit Flyer belongs to me. Or you might say I belong to it. You just don't understand how a Spirit Flyer really—"

"That's enough," Mrs. Bayley snapped. "I'll make a decision about this later. We need to be over at the school athletic field in ten minutes."

"What for?" Daniel asked. "School doesn't start yet."

"This is for the company sports league," Mrs. Bayley said. "I told you all about it. Goliath Industries always sponsors a sports league as a gesture of community good will when they move into a town. This time it's a soccer league."

"I don't want to play," Daniel said.

"Now, don't be difficult, Daniel," Mrs. Bayley said. "You'll have fun, and they'll be giving away free toys as a promotion."

"But I don't want to play soccer," Daniel said. "You have to run the entire time."

"Doctor Baker said you're perfectly able to run now," Mrs. Bayley said.

"But I'll still limp all over the place," Daniel said. "I'll look like a cripple out there."

"Don't say *cripple,*" Mrs. Bayley said. "You have to have a positive attitude, Daniel. You have a slight limp from an unfortunate accident. That's all. You can do everything the other kids do."

"That's easy for you to say," Daniel replied softly. He had had this same argument with his mother before, and he had always lost. And he knew he was going to lose again.

"You used to be the captain of your old soccer team, a real superstar, don't you remember?" Mrs. Bayley asked. She looked off in the distance for a moment as if she were looking back at a better time in life. "I know, I remember. I was so proud of you then. You'll get your confidence back. That's all that's holding you back."

Daniel started to say something else and then stopped. He knew it was no use. His mother was in a dream world of her own, he thought. She always wanted things to be the way they used to be before the accident. Since she was already mad because of the Spirit Flyer, he just kept quiet.

Mrs. Bayley locked up the house and garage. As they drove off, Denise and his mother were talking excitedly in the front seat. Daniel slouched down in the back.

"Every child in town will be signing up for the sports league," Mrs. Bayley said to Daniel, looking at him in the rearview mirror. "This will be a good way to meet people. Besides, it wouldn't look right if the children of Goliath's personnel manager didn't participate in the events sponsored by the company."

"That's the most important reason, isn't it?" Daniel asked.

Mrs. Bayley glared at her son. "Listen, Mr. Daniel Bayley," she said shrilly. "I know it's not easy to move to a new place and make new friends. But Goliath Industries pays the bills around here, and there's nothing wrong in showing a little appreciation and cooperation. To get along, you've got to go along. Got it?" Daniel just nodded and sat quietly the rest of the way to the school.

The parking lot at the Centerville school was packed. Daniel didn't think so many people could possibly live in Centerville. But then he figured some of the children lived on farms around the town. Daniel had never known anyone who lived on a farm. He had lived in a city or the suburbs all of his life. Mrs. Bayley got out of the car and immediately smiled and waved at someone she knew.

"Hurry up," she said to her children. "You need to mingle." Daniel and Denise got out of the car. Mrs. Bayley was smiling and saying hello to different people as they walked by. Daniel was surprised at the number of people his mother already knew. She was good at remembering names since it was part of her job as personnel manager.

Just then a whistle blew. A man in gym shorts and a jersey stood up on a platform. He wore a whistle around his neck. "That's Coach Carothers," Mrs. Bayley said. "We better go."

"I'll listen from here," Daniel said, moving under the shade of a large tree. Coach Carothers greeted everyone and then began explaining how the new sports league would work.

When the coach finally finished talking, Cyrus Cutright, the plant manager, stood up to speak. Daniel had seen Mr. Cutright before. He was a tall thin man with gray hair. His face was like leather and full of wrinkles. He seemed about a hundred and fifty years old and reminded Daniel of an old dried-up stick that could talk. But there was something in the eyes of Mr. Cutright that showed everyone he was the boss, even if he was old. His eyes could look right through you. Daniel didn't like to be around Mr. Cutright because he had seen those eyes up close once before and that was enough.

16

After Mr. Cutright sat down in a metal folding chair, an old woman named Mrs. Happy was introduced. She seemed kind, sort of like a grandmother or Mrs. Santa Claus. Daniel didn't pay attention until she mentioned the word *toys*. Then he listened. She was owner of the local toy store. She was going to give out some toys and some other things to all the newcomers.

Then another man stood up to speak. The top of his head was bald and he wore black-rimmed glasses. He was introduced as Mr. Smedlowe, the school principal. "I know I speak not only for Centerville School District but for the whole community as I welcome Goliath Industries and all the newcomers to our fair town," Mr. Smedlowe said.

The people began to applaud. Mr. Smedlowe smiled and applauded too. Finally, the clapping stopped. Mr. Smedlowe kept talking. Daniel leaned against the tree. He looked at all the people and wondered if it would be hard to make friends. Daniel had left two very good friends in the city. He knew he would miss them a lot. Daniel was remembering some of the bike rides he and his friends had gone on. Thinking about the Spirit Flyer, the boy was soon lost in his own thoughts.

The crowd's applause woke Daniel from his daydream. The people were walking over to rows of tables and lining up. He saw his mother waving at him. She wanted him to come to her. Daniel sighed and walked over. "You get in line at table number four," Mrs. Bayley said. "Denise is already over there. And please smile a little. People in a small town will think you're a snob if you don't smile."

Daniel limped over to the table where he saw Denise. The other kids watched him limping. Some began whispering to each other. Daniel looked down at his feet so he wouldn't see them. He got in line behind his sister. Denise was talking happily to the girl she had just met.

"I think he's the one," someone said behind Daniel. Daniel turned in time to see a boy with sandy brown hair get in line. The boy smiled in a friendly way. "My name's John," the boy said to Daniel. "You're new here, right?"

"Yeah. I'm Daniel," he replied.

A girl standing off to the side joined the line. She took off her glasses and looked at Daniel squarely in the eyes. She had brown hair and was a little taller than the boy. With or without glasses, Daniel thought she was quite pretty. He tried not to stare.

"This is Susan," John said. "She's my cousin."

"Hi," Daniel said. Daniel was about to say something else, when he reached the front of the line.

"I don't think you want to take one of those number cards," Susan whispered.

"What?" Daniel asked, puzzled. But before he could say anything else, his mother walked over. She pulled Daniel by his shoulders up to the woman behind the table. Daniel wanted to talk more to the new boy and girl, but he was locked in his mother's arms.

"Hello, Mrs. Happy, these are my children, Denise and Daniel," Mrs. Bayley said. "This is Mrs. Happy, the owner of the toy store here in Centerville. She sells a lot of Goliath toys."

"That's right," the old woman said with a smile. On her shoulder sat a black crow. Daniel blinked in surprise. "And this old bird is my friend, Nail."

"Oh," Daniel said. He looked closely at the old woman and crow. Something made him feel uneasy. Then he noticed the big black box behind the woman. The box seemed to be a five-foot cube. On the side facing the line was a large, three-foot white circle with a white X inside. The center of the X was a hole about the size of a soccer ball. Daniel stared at the white circled X and grew more and more uncomfortable.

"Why is that circled X on that thing?" Daniel asked.

"Just step right here," the old woman said as if she didn't hear Daniel's question. She gave both Denise and Daniel a black rectangular piece of plastic. "Put your number card in that slot and your face up to the hole. There will be a flash, like someone taking your picture. Then go around to the back and get your number card. Then you can go over to the truck and get your two free toys."

Denise put the odd black number card into the slot. When she put her face in the hole, there was a quick flash. Denise rubbed her eyes and walked behind the box. Daniel waited, staring at the circled X. His mother frowned at him. "Please hurry, young man," Mrs. Happy said. "Others are waiting."

"I don't want to," Daniel said softly. He tried to see the face of the new girl and boy he had just met, but his mother blocked his view.

"Daniel, don't be silly," his mother said. "The others are waiting."

"But you don't understand," Daniel replied. "I've seen the sign of the white circled X before."

"Come now, child, it only takes a second," the old woman said with a soothing smile. "And it doesn't hurt a bit."

"Why do I need a number card?" Daniel asked.

"All the children have them," Mrs. Happy said. "They are sort of like credit cards. You will need them to register on the Big Board too. So please hurry. We have more children to process."

"What's a Big Board?" the boy asked.

"Just do as you're told," Mrs. Bayley whispered angrily. "You're holding up the line."

Daniel looked at the smiling old woman and then at his frowning mother. He sighed and stepped forward. He put the piece of black plastic in the slot and his face up to the dark hole.

The flash made him see spots. He was still half-blinded as he walked around the back of the big box. A boy with black hair was putting something in a huge metal bin. He gave Daniel the number card. Daniel was surprised to see a shadowy image of his own face deep within the card. But what was even more surprising was that the face in the card was grinning. Daniel was sure he hadn't been smiling when he put his face up to the circled white X. He stared at the smiling face. Something deep inside the boy told him he had just made a big mistake.

AROUND TOWN

· · · · · · · · ·

2

Daniel looked around the crowds of people for the boy and girl he had just met, but they couldn't be found. Something about the girl's face lingered in his mind. He also wondered about her warning not to take the black number card.

He stared at the strange little card. It was the same size as a credit card and appeared to be made of black plastic. The shadowy image of Daniel's face was the oddest thing about the card. As Daniel stared at it he thought he saw the face actually change expression. He bent the card sideways for a closer look. Just then his mother grabbed his arm.

"Go ahead and pick up your free toys, Daniel," his mother said, pulling him along to a black truck that had the back doors open. The truck was stuffed with toys. A man looked at Daniel's number card, then waited.

"I'll take one of those and one of those," Daniel said.

"One Goliath Faster Blaster and Goliath Combo-Gizmo coming up," the man said. He put the toys in a bag and gave them to Daniel. "That's the only Combo-Gizmo we've given out. You got the last one."

"I saw some boys practicing soccer over by the bleachers," Mrs. Bayley said. "Why don't you go see if they'll let you play?"

"Oh, mother," Daniel groaned. "I don't know them."

"You need to mingle. Denise has already been invited to a party," Mrs. Bayley replied. She was about to say more, but then she saw Mr. Cutright. He was waving for her to come over.

Daniel felt relieved as his mother drifted away. He looked around. Everyone seemed to be doing something but him. Denise was talking to four other girls. Daniel saw that he could make an escape. Without looking at anyone, he walked through the parking lot away from the field. As he limped along, he felt as if the whole world must be watching. But he stared straight ahead. He was waiting to hear the voice of his mother calling him back, but the voice never came. He walked faster and faster until he was running in his limping gait. He didn't stop until the school was four blocks behind him and his escape was secure.

Though Daniel didn't know the streets very well, Centerville was an easy town to get around in. All the numbered streets, like Second and Tenth, ran east to west. All the named streets, like Oak and Maple, ran north and south. Main Street ran north and south through the middle of town. And at the very center of Centerville was the town square. The middle of the square held the county courthouse, as well as pretty trees and bushes and lots of grass. All along the sidewalk were old wooden rail benches. Most of the stores in Centerville lined the square, or were on North or South Main Street.

Main Street divided the town in halves of east and west. Since Daniel lived on Oak near West Fourteenth Street he knew he could find his way home. But first he wanted to explore. The south corner of the school ground was on East Tenth Street, which also ran out to the highway away from town. Daniel followed East Tenth all the way into the center of town.

The town square was a change for Daniel. Since he had lived in the city most of his life, he had usually gone to stores in big shopping centers or in big malls. He immediately liked the homey stores on the town square. He visited a music store, then looked at comic books in a drug store. When he saw a sign for the library, he made a beeline straight for it. The library was just off the southwest corner of the square on Tenth Street.

The wooden door to the library was old and worn; the brass doorknob was polished bright from so many hands turning it. When he stepped inside, he felt both at home and a little disappointed at the same time. He felt at home because the library had the familiar smell of books and papers and ink. Yet he was disappointed because the Centerville Library was much smaller than the one in his old neighborhood in the city.

The library seemed empty, so he didn't try to hide his limp. A woman was behind the counter. Even though he was sure she noticed his leg, she didn't ask him any questions like some people did. Adults, even total strangers, would often ask him how he hurt his leg as if they had a right to know just because he was a child and they were older. Daniel resented those kinds of questions, yet it was hard to be polite and not answer when someone asked.

He filled out a form and got a library card. Then he slowly walked up and down the rows of shelves, looking at all the books. He had read many of the books before, and he felt as if he were among friends. There were still plenty of books that looked interesting, so Daniel thought that maybe the library would be better than he first imagined. He finally checked out a book on World War 2 airplanes that he found in the adult nonfiction section and went back outside.

He walked around the town square once more, looking into the windows of all the stores. Then he walked up North Main to Fourteenth Street toward his home.

Daniel sighed with relief when he saw that his mother's car wasn't in the driveway. He got out his key and let himself in the front door. He ran upstairs, put the airplane book on his bed, then headed downstairs to the garage. The Spirit Flyer bicycle just seemed to be waiting for him. Daniel moved the Goliath Super Wings out of the way. He had only ridden the new bike a few times, and that was just to satisfy his mother.

His mother had really hoped he would forget all about the Spirit Flyer once she brought home the Super Wings. That's why she had wanted to leave his Spirit Flyer in storage at their old apartment complex and get it later. Daniel wondered if his mother really intended to get the bike at all. She had made it plain to Daniel several times how much she disapproved of the old bike.

The boy opened the small side door of the garage and rolled the Spirit Flyer outside. After he shut the door, he got on the bike. As he pedaled out into the street, he immediately began to feel better. Daniel had been both sad and worried about the move. Though he missed his friends, he missed his father more. Since his father still lived in the city, Daniel wondered how often he would see him. His father used to visit about every other weekend. But since they were living so far away now, he knew it would be even harder for them to visit each other.

Daniel pushed all the sad thoughts out of his mind as he rode the old red bicycle toward the edge of town. One of the best things about riding the bike was that no one noticed his limp. On two wheels, the injury became invisible, and Daniel felt free and normal. He pedaled north up Oak Street until most of the houses were gone.

Above Nineteenth Street, a two-lane road went west out of town. The sign said Cemetery Road. Daniel thought that was an unusual name, so he turned onto the road. As soon as he pedaled past the last house, he saw the big factory.

The factory was about a quarter of a mile down the road on the left. Two tall smokestacks stuck silently up into the sky. Since his mother worked there, Daniel thought he'd take a better look. A big chain-link fence surrounded the factory grounds. A small sign was stuck on the corner of the fence. The sign gave a warning:

Goliath Industries.

No Trespassing!!!

Enter at the Main Gate.

Barbed wire ran along the top of the tall fence. About every hundred feet, the same sign was posted. Daniel looked at the large dark buildings inside. He knew the factory was going to manufacture something for the government. His mother said it was part of a supersecret defense project.

He rode past the main driveway of the factory. A man in a uniform sat inside a little office by the gate. He stared at Daniel and then went back to his work. Daniel thought the factory was ugly. He kept pedaling. Beyond the factory to the south and west, Daniel could see machinery working on a parklike area. His mother had said that Goliath was building a country club and golf course next to the factory but that it wouldn't be completed until late September.

Daniel kept going west away from town. Not far past the factory he came to an old cemetery on the other side of the road. An arch was over the gate. Words inside the arch said: *Centerville Cemetery.* An iron fence surrounded the rows and rows of tombstones.

Daniel was just about to park the bike for a better look at the cemetery when it happened. The old red bicycle began to slowly move down Cemetery Road by itself. Daniel looked surprised and then smiled. This had happened several times before. He got a good grip on the handlebars and held on. That's when the handles of the handlebars moved down by themselves, aiming the handlebars up. The rolling front tire lifted off the asphalt and rose into the air, followed by the big back tire.

The bike glided silently up into the air as if it were following an invisible road into the sky.

The bike continued to pick up speed as it climbed higher and higher into the air. Daniel held on as the Spirit Flyer turned south. The boy and bike sailed toward a tall row of trees. But long before he got to the forest, the bicycle was at least twenty feet higher than the highest treetop. Daniel smiled again. As the bike sailed up into the sky, a fresh feeling of freedom filled the boy. There was nothing like riding his old Spirit Flyer! Though he didn't really understand how the mysterious old bicycle worked, he didn't care. Soaring above the trees and fields was enough.

The bicycle turned again as it rose up near the clouds. Daniel crossed over a muddy brown river that looked like a mere ribbon far below. Then the bike suddenly shot forward in the sky. The ride was smooth and the wind felt crisp and cool and seemed to wash all the sadness off the boy.

He felt relieved that the Spirit Flyer still worked. He had been worried that the move might have damaged the old bike. Daniel had wanted to wrap the Spirit Flyer in a blanket and put it on top of the family car, but his mother had been dead set against it. And when his mother had said he couldn't even take it in the moving truck, Daniel felt worse than any time since right after the car accident. But during the long argument before the move, the old bicycle seemed to be telling Daniel not to worry.

The only thing Daniel knew for sure was that the Spirit Flyer was full of surprises. Each ride held its own adventure, and each time he felt as if he learned just a little more about the secrets the old bicycle contained. From experience, he had learned to go with the flow of the Spirit Flyer. Though he didn't know where the bicycle was taking him, he had confidence that he was ok. In one sense, he was more and more lost as the bicycle carried him away from town. But in another sense, Daniel felt more at home on the seat of the old bicycle than anywhere else.

Daniel smiled high above the world. He began humming a song to himself. The words of the song were about kings and wind and light. Some of his friends with Spirit Flyers had taught him the song. He was still singing when the bicycle began to glide back down toward the earth. The boy and bike seemed to be out in the middle of nowhere. All he could see was forest and trees and more trees.

As they passed over a dirt road, the bike zoomed closer to the ground, just below the branches of a huge oak tree. He skimmed along just three feet above the road, then softly touched down. That's when he saw a driveway and a gate ahead. The bike turned inside the driveway and slowly rolled to a halt.

Daniel surveyed the scene. Ahead of him was a white house with blue shutters. The house seemed abandoned or poorly kept up since the grass was very tall in the yard. Off to the left was another long white building like a garage or workshop. It had two big blue doors on the front. Then Daniel heard voices.

In a flash, he got off the old red bike and pushed it behind a tree. He peeked out from behind the trunk and then laid the bike down in the tall grass.

He was confused, wondering why the old bicycle had brought him to this place. He took a deep breath and walked from behind the tree toward the white building next to the house. His limp was hardly noticeable as he waded through the tall grass.

The voices got louder as he approached the blue doors. He was about twenty feet away when everything got quiet. Just then, the doors burst open. A boy walked out, followed by a girl. Daniel recognized them immediately. They were the same two children who had been behind him in the line at the school right before he got his number card.

When the children saw Daniel, they stopped. The boy with sandy hair looked at Daniel, then frowned.

"What are you doing here?" he demanded. "This is private property."

"John, don't be so mean," the girl said. She pushed back her rich brown hair and smiled at Daniel. "I'm sorry. He doesn't mean it."

"Yes, I do," the boy insisted. "What are you doing out here?"

"I was just riding my bike," Daniel said.

"Way out here?" the other boy asked. "You're eight miles away from town. Did you know that?"

"Well, I wasn't quite sure of the road miles," Daniel replied. He cleared his throat and felt more uncomfortable by the second. "But I can leave. I didn't really mean to trespass or anything. It's just that . . . well, never mind."

Daniel turned around. He began walking for the gate. He heard the children talking.

"I think you're being mean to him," the girl said.

"But why is he snooping out here?" the boy asked. "He was in line with all the others. He took a number card. I don't like it. Look, he's kind of crippled or something."

"Shhhhhh," the girl said. "You'll hurt his feelings."

Daniel walked quickly into the tall grass trying not to let his limp show. He felt as if his ears were burning as red as his red hair. He got to the gate and looked back. They were still watching him. Daniel waited. He knew he should get the old red bicycle, but something told him to be afraid. He was already embarrassed and felt a little angry at his bike for bringing him to a place where he got in trouble.

Then Daniel thought of a plan, a sort of lie, really. He walked through the gate as if he had left his bicycle out in the road. He walked out of sight. Then he scrunched down and crept back toward the house. He peeked from behind a tree. The boy and girl were still standing by the big blue doors, and they appeared to be arguing. Finally, the boy went back inside and so did the girl. She shut the door behind her.

Daniel immediately scrambled back around through the gate and ran for the Spirit Flyer still hidden in the grass. The old red bicycle seemed to weigh a ton as he struggled to lift it. "Come on!" Daniel whispered. He yanked and yanked, but he felt as if he were lifting an elephant. The old bicycle seemed to be resisting on purpose. Sweat popped out on Daniel's forehead. Just then, he gave a tremendous yank and the bicycle finally rose up on both tires.

Daniel was about to hop on the bicycle for a quick getaway. But when he looked up, the two children were standing ten feet away and staring at him. The boy looked surprised. The brown-haired girl was staring at his bicycle. Daniel knew his face was beet red. He felt like his freckles must be blinking off and on like neon lights, advertising how embarrassed he felt.

"I'm trying to leave," Daniel mumbled. "Really, I am."

He pushed the old bike forward through the grass, but it would hardly move. He felt like he was pushing it through mud. He looked at the children. The girl looked right into his eyes, and then she smiled. Daniel shuddered under her stare.

"Please don't go," she said. "My name is Susan Kramar, and this is my cousin, John Kramar. And anyone with a Spirit Flyer is welcome here."

DANIEL'S NEW FRIENDS

· · · · · · · · ·

3

Daniel stood in the tall grass, holding onto the handlebars of the old red bicycle, looking down at his feet. If he could have run away, he would have since he felt so embarrassed. But he realized the Spirit Flyer wasn't moving anywhere soon, and he knew enough to stick with the old bike. He still had the feeling his freckles must be glowing on and off. Finally he felt enough courage to look up into the eyes of the brown-haired girl.

She was still smiling. Daniel didn't understand such a mysterious smile. The girl seemed very old, like a woman for an instant, and then once again just a girl. Daniel thought she was extremely pretty. Just thinking that made him feel funny inside. He couldn't describe the feeling. More than anything, he felt the same old embarrassment and fear he usually had around people.

"I'll go away," Daniel said. He pushed on the bike again. "Really, I will. Just as soon as this . . . bike . . . will . . . roll . . ."

"I don't think you're going anywhere," the girl said with a smile. She almost seemed to be laughing. "But I bet if you push it toward the house, it will roll. Try it."

Daniel shrugged his shoulders. Not knowing what else to do, he turned the bike toward the house. As soon as he pushed, the tires rolled easily. Daniel looked at the girl with new respect, wondering how she knew. "Come on," Susan said. She waved him forward. John was walking by her.

Daniel followed them. Every so often, the girl would look back and smile encouragingly. Her smile made him feel good, yet nervous too. Daniel hoped some of the redness was leaving his face. He was glad that the bicycle hid his limp. The children stopped at the two big blue doors of the long white building.

"You can leave your bike there," the girl said. "Come, let me show you something." Daniel knocked down the kickstand with his foot. John opened one of the big blue doors and went inside. Susan walked over to the door and waited. "Come on," she urged and smiled again.

Daniel walked forward, immediately aware of his limp. He felt hot all over again under her gaze. He knew he was turning red and hated himself for it, which only made it worse.

He looked down and walked into the cool shade of the building. Still looking down, the first thing he saw were two big balloon tires of bicycle wheels on the cement floor. Daniel's heart leaped as he looked up and saw not only one but two old red bicycles. His face became a big grin when he saw the names, *Spirit Flyer,* in the familiar white letters. He walked over and looked below the center of the handlebars. He smiled. Three golden crowns linked together were stuck right into the metal. Daniel touched them softly. The crowns were a sign the bicycles were indeed genuine Spirit Flyers.

"You knew," he said to them. "You have Spirit Flyers too."

"Anyone with a Spirit Flyer can't be all bad," Susan said. "Right, John?"

"That's right," the boy said. "I'm sorry if I was a little rough on you before. I guess I was surprised to see anyone out here. And since you're new in town, we just didn't know. A lot of changes have been happening in Centerville lately, and they haven't been good."

"What do you mean?" Daniel asked.

"Come have some ice tea first," Susan said. "I bet you're thirsty." The children were in a small front room, rather like a hallway. But a door was opened to another room beyond. Susan led the way. Daniel followed the two children. The room was huge and took up the rest of the building. A long workbench ran down most of one wall. Boxes covered with dust were lying all around the room everywhere Daniel looked.

A space had been cleared on a section of the workbench. A big green-and-white jug sat on the edge near some empty pint canning jars. Susan held an empty canning jar up to the spout at the bottom of the jug and pushed the little button. Tea squirted into the glass container. When the pint jar was nearly full, she gave it to Daniel. He took a long drink and suddenly realized how thirsty he had been. The tea was cold and refreshing. He drank half of it in one long gulp.

"Have a seat," Susan said. Both she and John sat down backwards in old wooden chairs so their arms were folded over the upright back of the chair. Daniel sat down on a stool near the workbench. He looked around the large room once more. In one corner, big power tools covered in dust and cobwebs stood silently on heavy metal legs. The room was like his old school's industrial arts workshop.

"Where did you get your Spirit Flyer?" John asked Daniel.

"In the city where I used to live, I had a friend named Dirk whose whole family had Spirit Flyers," Daniel said. "They moved to the same apartment complex about four months ago. They used to go out riding on Sundays and asked me along. I didn't believe they really flew and all like my friend had said. I thought they were just ugly old bikes. But I went along. Anyway, we went out to the country to this campground. And sure enough, when they got on the bicycles, away they flew, right up into the air. I couldn't believe it."

"I know just the feeling you mean," Susan said with a smile. "Our family has Spirit Flyers, but we've still only ridden all together as a family just four or five times. The feeling is even more special when you ride together like that. But my parents always seem too busy."

"Or too afraid," John added with an impatient frown.

"Well, I was real scared the first time I rode one," Daniel admitted. "Anyway, they gave me a ride and told me about the Three Kings and told me I could have a Spirit Flyer free for the asking. I really wanted one, but then I saw the chains for the first time."

"We know about those chains," Susan said, nodding her head.

"I didn't even realize I had a chain until they showed me," Daniel said. "My friend, Dirk, flipped on the old light on his bike, and I looked down and sure enough, there was the chain right around my neck. And it was locked with this big dark lock. That's when they began telling me about the Three Kings and Treason and the war going on in the Deeper World. At first I thought it was all some kind of fairy tale. But the more they talked, the more it all made sense. Nothing else could explain the chain or the power of the Spirit Flyers. I was pretty confused. I hardly slept that night or the rest of that week. But I could sure feel the chain, just as much as I could feel the limp in my leg, only worse. Deep down, I finally realized how much of a slave I was to the chain. I asked the Three Kings to free me from the chain. I woke up the next morning and found the Spirit Flyer right in my bedroom! When I rolled the bike into the kitchen, my mother was full of questions. I told her the whole story, but she didn't believe me. She still thinks I'm just pretending or something. She has never believed a word I've said about my Spirit Flyer."

"I know that feeling," John Kramar said, nodding his head sympathetically. Susan smiled. Daniel felt more at ease. Besides Dirk, his family and two other boys, Daniel hadn't known any other people with Spirit Flyers.

"You said your mom and dad are divorced?" Susan asked.

"Yeah," Daniel said.

"That's too bad," Susan said, sensing the red-headed boy's pain.

"My mom and dad disappeared in a storm when I was four years old," John said. "Everyone says a tornado got them. All they found was their car, all smashed up. I've lived with Susan's family ever since."

Daniel shuddered. He suddenly felt sorry for him. At least my parents are alive, Daniel thought.

"I was in a car crash too, about three years ago," Daniel said. "That's how I hurt my leg. A drunk driver ran through a red light and hit us. My right leg got crushed. The end of the bone was injured and didn't grow right. So now that leg is shorter than my regular left leg. I used to be pretty good at sports, but not anymore."

"That's a shame," Susan said. Daniel looked at her. Her face was filled with concern.

"Thanks," Daniel said, not sure why he said it. "My dad was hurt in the car wreck too. He really hurt his hip bone. His hip got better, but he was never quite the same. Everything seemed to change. He and my mom just didn't get along. I don't know why it all happened."

Daniel stopped talking. He felt uncomfortable talking about his parents and their problems. He knew his mother wouldn't like it if he said too much about their family to total strangers. Yet Daniel didn't feel the two children were strangers at all since they had Spirit Flyers.

"This is my mom and dad's old workshop," John Kramar told Daniel. "They had Spirit Flyers too. And so do our grandfather and grandmother. They know a lot about the Three Kings and the Deeper World and all sorts of things."

"Grandfather Kramar was the one who gave us our copy of *The Book of the Kings,*" the girl added.

"Dirk's family gave me my copy," Daniel said. "You can buy them almost anywhere, though. Do you guys have a pair of Spirit Flyer Vision goggles? I got a pair a few weeks ago."

"They can really help you see deeper into things," Susan said and smiled. John Kramar nodded. Daniel took another gulp of ice tea. The room was suddenly quiet.

"By the way, why did you guys disappear at the school this morning?" Daniel asked.

"Because of that creepy Mrs. Happy, that's why," Susan Kramar said. Her whole face changed in an instant.

"She was giving out number cards again, and those free Goliath Toys," John added.

"What's wrong with that?" Daniel asked. He pulled the black number card out of his pocket. He stared down at the dark image of his own face on the black plastic. "I picked out a couple of toys too since they were free and all."

The two Kramar children looked back and forth at each other. Daniel began to feel uncomfortable. "She processed you too, didn't she?" Susan asked. "She must have processed every new kid in town today."

"Everyone has these cards from what I understand," Daniel said. "Don't you guys?"

The two Kramar children exchanged glances again. Daniel thought they were being overly secretive. "We still have the cards," Susan said slowly. "We tried to destroy them, first with the lights on the Spirit Flyers, then by burning them and cutting them up. Nothing works. They always come back."

"What do you mean?" Daniel asked.

"You can't get rid of them," John replied with a sigh. "I've thrown mine away a hundred times and each time it just comes back. They just appear on your dresser or inside your pocket. There's something wrong with those cards. We don't know exactly how they work, but it's like they are little pieces of darkness from the Deeper World."

"I thought I saw the face on mine move," Daniel said.

"Your face moved too?" John asked. "I bet it's the ghostslave. I knew it. Susan has never seen it since her face was never put on the card."

"I thought that old woman said they were some kind of identification card," Daniel said. "What do you mean about ghostslaves? I read about ghostslaves in *The Book of the Kings,* but I didn't quite understand what they were."

"Ghostslaves are sort of like the person you used to be before you got your Spirit Flyer," Susan said. "But they are still in the deeper chains, and they try to control you. They don't really have any power, unless you give it to them. Then you've got trouble."

"How do you give them power?" Daniel asked.

"It's kind of tricky," John said. "Ghosts can only scare you if you believe in them and believe they can hurt you. Ghostslaves are sort of the same. You make them come to life by being afraid of them. They shake the chain and try to make you think you were never freed from the deeper chains yourself."

"But it's all lies and tricks because we are free in the Kingdom of the Kings," Susan added. "Only sometimes, you don't *feel* free. That's when ghostslaves really try to control you. It's all a part of the battle going on in the Deeper World. Neither one of us quite understands how the number cards work, but I think they're made of the same material as those black windows that Mrs. Happy has in her store."

"Black windows?" Daniel asked.

"Well, they aren't really windows like a regular window," John answered. "They're sort of like holes or passageways into the Deeper World. And we think the number cards are made of the same material. And since every kid in town has them, we think she's going to use them in some sort of bad way. Only we don't know what it is yet, or how to fight it."

Daniel pulled the small number card out of his pocket. He looked closely at the shadowy reflection of his face. Though something about the card gave him a creepy feeling, he wondered if the Kramar children were just exaggerating.

"There's also something wrong with those toys she gives out, in a deeper way," Susan said. "And there's something wrong with Goliath Industries too, if you ask me. All of this is part of a deeper attack, like the battles mentioned in *The Book of the Kings*. I think the whole town of Centerville is in for a lot of trouble with Goliath opening up that factory."

"What do you mean?" Daniel asked. "My mother works for Goliath Industries. She thinks it's the best job she's ever had. And what's wrong with the Goliath Toys?" Daniel suddenly felt defensive because of his mother. Even though he didn't get along that well with her, it still hurt him to think of his newly found friends not liking the place where she worked.

As he thought of his mother, he suddenly remembered to look at his watch. It was almost one o'clock. Daniel couldn't believe how quickly the time had gone. "I've got to go," he said suddenly. He drank the rest of the ice tea and set the empty jar on the bench. "I was supposed to be home for lunch a half-hour ago. She'll really be mad." Daniel rushed for the door. He forgot all about his limp. He was already on his Spirit Flyer by the time the Kramar kids caught up with him.

"We can talk later," Susan said. She smiled, but Daniel thought he saw something new in her face, some kind of doubt. He hoped he was just imagining what he saw.

"See you," Daniel said. He began pedaling the old red bike. He aimed the handlebars toward the sky and the tires lifted quietly into the air. Daniel waved back at the children on the ground and then shot higher into the sky. When he was above all the trees, he saw the two smoke-stacks of the Goliath Industries factory and the water tower of Center-ville. He stood up on the pedals of the old bicycle and the Spirit Flyer jumped forward in a hum.

Back on the ground, near the workshop, Susan and John Kramar watched him shoot out of sight. "He was in a hurry," John said.

"I hope he doesn't get in trouble," Susan said.

"Well, maybe his mom will understand," John replied.

"I don't mean that," the girl said. "I mean with the number card and those Goliath toys. He doesn't really know the dangers yet. He didn't seem to know what the ghostslave can do to you." Susan twisted a strand of her brown hair as she stared into the sky where she had last seen her new friend.

"He'll find out soon enough, I imagine," John replied. "Let's get back to work. Maybe we can find something in my mom and dad's stuff that can help all of us, like more of those keys."

Susan nodded. She followed her cousin back to the workshop. She looked into the sky once more and then closed the big blue doors behind them.

BARRY'S
OLD
FRIENDS

. . . .

4

Daniel knew he was in trouble the minute he saw his mother's face. He had parked the Spirit Flyer in the garage quietly, but his mother was waiting right by the door when he came in.

"Where have you been, young man?" Mrs. Bayley demanded.

"I was just out riding my Spirit Flyer," Daniel said. His mother frowned.

"I knew it! We're not even here one day and you're out . . . pretending on that stupid bicycle. It's bad enough that you ran off from your first opportunity to meet new friends. But you also had to be late and scare me half to death. Your lunch is cold."

"I did meet some new friends," Daniel said. "And guess what? They each have Spirit Flyers too."

Mrs. Bayley looked hard at him. Daniel knew he had made another mistake the instant the words were out of his mouth. His mother hadn't approved of his old friends with Spirit Flyers. She had even called up Dirk's mother and complained about the Spirit Flyers and all sorts of things. She had told Dirk's mom that she didn't want them filling Daniel's head with a bunch of nonsense and fairy tales about a bunch of silly old bicycles. Daniel had thought he would die of embarrassment because his mother had caused such a scene.

"I'm very disappointed in you, Daniel," his mother said slowly. "You know how I feel about that junky old bicycle. You will mix socially with the children of this town, the normal children. Who are the names of these so-called friends of yours?"

Daniel was quiet. He looked down at his feet.

"What were their names, young man?" his mother repeated. "No use in lying to me."

"Good grief," Daniel blurted out. "I'm not lying. I hadn't said a word."

"Just tell me their names, then," Mrs. Bayley said.

"Susan and John Kramar," Daniel said.

Mrs. Bayley cocked her head, thinking for a moment. Then she shrugged her shoulders. "Well, their parents don't work at the factory," she said. "But the name *Kramar* sounds familiar. Daniel, I want you to meet other children. You used to be such a good mixer and got along so well, like Denise. That's why I've accepted an invitation to the Smedlowe's party this evening."

"Mother!" Daniel wailed. "I don't want to go to a party."

"That is precisely why I accepted for you," Mrs. Bayley said. She turned and went back into the house. Daniel followed close behind.

"Are you just going to run my whole life?" Daniel demanded.

"I'm only trying to give you some social skills that you badly lack," Mrs. Bayley said. "Sometimes you're as bad as your father."

Daniel felt a stab of pain inside, as if he'd been punched in the stomach. He hated it when his mother started criticizing his father. "What does Dad have to do with me going to a party in Centerville?" Daniel grumbled.

"Nothing, except that he had no social skills whatsoever, either," Mrs. Bayley replied. "Besides not having any ambition, he couldn't have advanced in a real career even if he wanted. And you want to know why? Because he had no social skills, that's why."

He wondered if his mother was right. His father was an educated man. He had a master's degree in engineering, but he worked as a custodian in a big office building. His father had lost several well-paying jobs because he was hard to work with, at least that's what his mother always said.

"He just didn't believe in buttering up people," Daniel said defensively.

"The sooner you learn in life who butters the bread, the better off you'll be, young man," Mrs. Bayley replied. "You've got to present your good points and show you're a winner. When I hire people, it's because they look like winners. Your father has that loser image. He doesn't cooperate. I wouldn't hire him to work for me, even as a janitor. Not a chance."

"That's probably why he left us," Daniel muttered. He knew the instant he said it that he had made a big mistake.

"What did you say?" Mrs. Bayley asked slowly. Daniel looked down at the carpet. His mother grabbed him by the chin so he had to look her in her eyes. "I asked you a question."

"Nothing," Daniel sighed. "It doesn't matter anyway."

"I don't like your attitude, Daniel Bayley," his mother said, her voice cracking. Then suddenly she began to cry. Daniel swallowed, watching his mother. As soon as the tears came, an awful, terrible feeling settled over him in a suffocating wave. He hated it when his mother cried. Ever since the divorce she seemed to swing so quickly in her moods. Most of the time she acted strong and capable and professional, almost as if she was more a manager at home than a mother. At other times she just seemed to fall apart, like a flimsy toy. Daniel couldn't figure her out.

"I'm sorry, Mom," Daniel said. His mother covered her face with her hands and sobbed. Her shoulders shook. Daniel wanted to comfort her and take back the mean words, but he knew it was too late. He felt sick at his stomach watching his mother sob. After a few minutes, she wiped her eyes. Her make-up was smeared as she looked Daniel in the eyes.

"Your father is an intelligent person. I give him credit for that," her mother sniffled. "And you have even more brains, according to the school tests. But intelligence isn't worth a red cent if you can't get along with people. I'm trying to do the best I can with you children. That's why I accepted the invitation to the party for you. Believe me, someday you'll thank me for pushing you out of the nest so you'd learn how to fly."

I already know how to fly, Daniel thought to himself. But he had his Spirit Flyer in mind.

"Are you going to cooperate or not?" Mrs. Bayley asked. Daniel looked at his mother's tear-stained face and knew there was only one answer. All he wanted at that moment was to make his mother happy again. He nodded his head slowly.

"The party is at five o'clock," she sniffed. "I want you to wear nice clothes. Denise is going too. The Smedlowes have practically the nicest house in Buckingham Estates. His mother comes from a wealthy family, I understand. So I want you to look sharp. Take your swimming suit. The Smedlowes have a boy close to your age and I think he's even the president of his own little club. If you're lucky enough for him to ask you to join, do it."

"Now I have to join the club of some kid I don't even know?" Daniel whined. He would have complained louder but he was afraid his mother would start crying again.

"You used to like being popular. Don't you remember?" Mrs. Bayley sniffed. She went to a mirror over the fireplace and frowned when she saw the stains in her make-up. She took a compact out of her purse and began repairing the damage. "We may be moving up into Buckingham Estates one of these days ourselves. You might as well be in the clubs of the same neighborhood children and same social position. Now go eat your lunch and be ready at quarter till five."

Daniel was dressed and pressed by quarter till five just like his mother had commanded. Though it wasn't far to the Smedlowes, Mrs. Bayley drove the car. Buckingham Estates was an area on the southwest corner of town. The lots were big, with houses of stone and brick. All the yards were very green and neat. Shiny new cars filled the driveways. Some of the yards had fancy iron fences and gates.

The Smedlowe's house was the second biggest house in the neighborhood. A new house just across the street from the Smedlowes was the biggest house on the block. Mrs. Bayley parked in front of this house. Men with tool belts were scurrying in and out the front door.

"That's the house of Mr. Favor," Daniel's mother said as they came to a stop. "He's the executive vice president out at the factory. He'll be moving his family into Centerville soon."

A maid let the Bayleys into the Smedlowe house. All the people were in the back yard. Children were splashing and playing water basketball in the pool. The adults were sitting at little tables with umbrellas as they sipped on drinks.

Daniel tried to hide his limp as he walked closely behind his mother and sister. His mother immediately began greeting all sorts of people and smiling. She had such an easy, ready smile when she wanted, Daniel thought. That's what she meant by social skills. Denise was a lot like his mom. Besides being pretty, she seemed comfortable talking to anyone and made friends easily. Since the accident, Daniel always felt awkward meeting new people.

Just then, a boy with wet black hair pulled himself up out of the pool and came over to Daniel. "I'm Barry Smedlowe," he said, smiling real big. The water dripped down his face and legs. "If you've got a swimming suit, get it on and you can be on our team. We're just getting ready to play another game of water basketball. You can change in the bathhouse."

"Sure," Daniel said. He liked the water. No one could notice his limp when he was in water. In fact, everyone looked like they limped a little themselves when they tried to walk in water. Daniel changed, then walked quickly to the pool. He tried his best not to limp. He also hoped none of the other kids would notice the two long purplish scars near the bottom of his right leg. He jumped quickly into the water.

"You can be on my team," Barry said. "It's me and Doug and Freddie and Mike and Roger against those guys."

The other boys smiled and said hello. Daniel smiled back.

"You live just two houses down from me," the boy named Doug said. "I recognized you by your hair. I don't think anyone in Centerville has hair as red as yours."

"Probably not," Daniel said, trying to be nice. He was used to people teasing him about his hair.

"Let's play!" Barry shouted. He grabbed the basketball bobbing on top of the water and passed to Freddie. The game began.

Though Daniel was nervous at first, he did ok. He made several baskets and even intercepted a few passes. Thirty minutes into the game, he knew he had passed the first test among the boys. No matter where you went, it was always the same—you had to prove you were good at games or else you were in trouble. Daniel hated having to prove anything, but it didn't matter. He did it anyway. That's what his mother meant by social skills. Deep down, Daniel had to admit he wanted to be accepted by the other boys. Before the accident, he had been one of the most popular kids in his class. Like his mother, he hadn't forgotten those days. Life had seemed so much easier then. Every so often, Daniel would look up and see his mother watching him. She smiled with great approval as she saw him getting along with the other boys.

Seeing that smile meant a lot to the boy.

Sooner or later, Daniel knew he would have to get out of the pool. He played the game heartily, wishing it would last until dark. Then the other children wouldn't notice his limp and ugly scars on his leg. But Daniel knew it was useless to try to hide in the water forever.

Around six o'clock, the boys stopped playing to eat the grilled hamburgers Mr. Smedlowe had cooked. Daniel was the last person out of the water and realized he had made a mistake by waiting. All the other boys stopped and stared as they saw Daniel limp across the deck to the bathhouse. Daniel felt his ears turning red, but he couldn't help it. He saw some of the boys whispering. Though he couldn't really hear, he knew what they were whispering about.

After he got his regular clothes on, Daniel walked back over to the group. He wondered if he should have just stayed in his bathing suit like the other boys, but then they would see the ugly scars on his leg. He avoided the eyes of the other boys and limped toward the table of food. He filled his plate carefully.

All the other boys had their food and were sitting at a table away from the adults. Barry smiled and waved for Daniel to come over. Daniel braced himself and limped toward them.

"Sit here," Barry said, pointing to a lawn chair.

Daniel sat back and before he knew it, he was falling backward as the chair collapsed. The plate of food tipped up and over on his chest. The hot baked beans were the worst, but the ketchup and mustard on his cheeseburger bun were almost as sticky.

The other boys hooted and howled in laughter as they looked at Daniel. Barry was laughing the hardest, in a loud braying voice. All the adults had stopped talking and were staring. Mr. Smedlowe frowned and walked over. Daniel struggled to get up, but his hand slipped on the beans and bunless cheeseburger, which only made the other boys laugh harder. Barry was holding his sides and his eyes were wet because he was laughing so hard.

"What's going on here?" Mrs. Smedlowe demanded. "Who let Daniel sit in this chair? Barry, you knew this chair was broken."

"I just forgot, Daddy," Barry said, and shrugged his shoulders. He stuck out his hand to help Daniel up. But Daniel refused it. He felt a surge of anger welling up inside.

"I'll get a roll of paper towels and some more food," Mr. Smedlowe said to Daniel. "Barry, I just hope this was an accident. Look at the mess on Daniel's shirt and pants."

"It was an accident, Daddy," Barry said. His face couldn't have looked more innocent if he were a baby.

Daniel stood there, the food still oozing down his shirt. The other boys covered their mouths with their hands, trying to hide their giggles.

"Sorry about the chair, Danny," Barry said. "I guess I forgot it was broken."

"Sure," Daniel said, trying to control his anger. Mr. Smedlowe returned with a roll of paper towels, a new chair and a plate of food. Daniel wiped up the mess on himself as Mr. Smedlowe cleaned the food off the ground. Daniel saw his mother frowning from a distance. Finally Mr. Smedlowe left. The other boys began eating and talking again, ignoring Daniel. They talked mostly about the new sports league that Goliath Industries was sponsoring.

"Well, I'm going to make the Superstar team for sure," Barry announced to the others, even though his mouth was full of food. Daniel looked away. He was glad that he was being ignored.

"I hope I make the team too," Doug Barns said. "I heard we can win more free toys."

"And get Goliath Credit Points too," Freddie added. "But what are they, anyway?"

"I'm not exactly sure how they work, but Mrs. Happy said she'd tell me next week," Barry said confidently. "You need the points to get more stuff, I think. The points are sort of like money. I want to use my points to get a new bike. Goliath has a bike called a Goliath Super Wings and

I want one. I heard they're really great."

Daniel looked up. He had finished his food quickly. He stood up and started to walk away but stopped and said, "I don't know if Super Wings are all that great," Daniel said.

"How would you know, Food Face?" Barry demanded. He looked at the other boys and they all giggled.

"Yeah, Red, how would you know?" Alvin added. The boys grinned like goons.

"Because I have a Super Wings," Daniel said simply. Then he turned and walked away.

"Big deal," Doug said. "So what if he has one? And will you look at that limp?"

"Yeah, Gimpy the Limpy," Mike said.

Daniel stiffened as he walked. The words felt like stinging stones hitting his back. The other boys kept laughing—all except Barry. He silently watched Daniel limping away.

"Shut up!" Barry hissed to the others.

"What's the matter with you?" Doug asked.

"Yeah, why are you sticking up for Gimpy?"

"I want him to join the Cobra Club," Barry said.

"What?" the other boys demanded in unison.

"I want him to join the club," Barry said evenly. "And I'm calling an emergency meeting right now. We'll meet out in my garage."

Daniel was sitting on the end of a lawn chair near his sister and his mother when he saw the boys all get up and leave together like a pack of dogs.

"I think I'll go home and change," Daniel whispered to his mother.

"What about your new friends?" she asked. "Don't you want to play with them some more?"

"Not looking like this," Daniel said, pointing at his shirt and pants. "I'll walk home. It's not far."

"I guess that's ok," his mother said slowly. "Come on back when you get your clean clothes."

Daniel nodded wearily. Then he limped past the crowd of people, avoiding their eyes. Once he was past the wooden gate that led out to the street, he began to run. He ran to the street and then ran faster. His short leg clomped like a stick, but Daniel kept on running. Yet even at his fastest, he couldn't outrun the tears that began to fill his eyes. The street began to get blurry, but Daniel still ran.

JOIN
THE
CLUB
· · · · · · · · ·
5

Monday morning started the first regular work week for the Bayley family. Daniel's mother had hired an older woman named Mrs. Jenkins to clean house and watch the children part of the day. Daniel thought he was too old to be watched by a baby sitter, but his mother insisted it was only until school started in the fall. Daniel didn't have to stay at home the whole day, so that gave him at least some satisfaction.

"These Goliath toys are valuable," Denise said at breakfast on Monday morning.

"Of course they're valuable," Mrs. Bayley replied.

"I don't just mean price," Denise explained. "They're kind of like collector's items here in Centerville. Most all the kids are collecting them. They're real popular and in style. I heard Barry Smedlowe has the biggest collection of Goliath toys. He bought up every Combo-Gizmo in town supposedly. No one knows why."

"I have one," Daniel said. He hadn't even taken the odd-looking toy out of the box.

"The first practice of the new sports league is this evening," Denise said.

"Well, I want both of you to be on time," Mrs. Bayley said. "I also have some good news. I found out that Daniel is on the same team as Barry and the other boys in his club. But that's not the best news. Mrs. Smed-lowe brunched with us yesterday morning, and she said Barry wants you to join his little club."

"Are you kidding?" Daniel asked. "Barry set me up in that broken chair."

"But that was just an accident," his mother said.

"No, it wasn't," Daniel replied. Since his mother was supposed to know so much about other people's characters, Daniel couldn't under-stand why his mother didn't see right through a guy like Barry.

"Well, even if the boys were having a little fun, you shouldn't take it so personally," Mrs. Bayley said. "You're too sensitive. Boys your age like to tease each other. It's like a game. You should just play along and act like those things don't bother you."

"I'd like to see you play along with a plateful of hot baked beans and a cheeseburger on your chest," Daniel grunted. "I don't like their kinds of games."

"Don't get a sour attitude before you give them a chance," Mrs. Bayley instructed.

"I'm getting out of here," Denise said. "I hate to hear you two argue."

"I'm discussing. Daniel is arguing," Mrs. Bayley said as Denise walked out of the kitchen.

"I met some people I like, the Kramar kids, but you don't want me to give them a chance," Daniel accused. He had been thinking of Susan Kramar all weekend. He kept seeing her face and mysterious smile.

"That's a different matter altogether," Mrs. Bayley said, sitting up straight. Her voice took on a businesslike tone. "I've been asking around about those children. Their father is the sheriff here. He's rubbed a few of the more important people in town the wrong way. The Smedlowes think Centerville needs a new sheriff. So those Kramar kids might not even be around town past the next election. That's only a few months away. So you might as well make friends with kids who are going to be here, like the kids in Buckingham Estates."

"Because they have a lot of money, right?" Daniel asked.

"It's not just money," Mrs. Bayley said. "I want you to be able to thrive in the right atmosphere. People act like their friends and if you have friends with low standards, then you adopt low standards yourself. That's just a social fact of life."

"And you think joining a club with a bunch of jerky guys will give me high standards?" Daniel asked.

"All I'm saying is that you have to expect children to play a few tricks on newcomers. That's just the way the game of life is played, like it or not."

"But, I don't want to play with—"

"Don't use that tone of voice with me, young man," his mother said crossly. "I've done some thinking, and ever since you got that junky old bicycle you've gotten a bad attitude. You used to like being popular and having a lot of friends. I have a good mind to just take that junky old bicycle to the dump where it belongs."

"You can't do that," Daniel almost shouted.

"Oh, yes. I can," Mrs. Bayley replied firmly. By the look in her eyes, Daniel could see that she meant it. "I have legal custody of you children, and I can raise you as I see fit. I think that bike is unhealthy for you. I'm tempted to just go call the junkman right now."

Daniel was speechless with fear. He knew his mother didn't like the Spirit Flyer, but he didn't think she'd try to go that far. He felt his face getting hot. "You wouldn't really do that," Daniel stammered. He couldn't think straight.

"Oh, no?" his mother asked.

"I would go live with Dad," Daniel said in desperation. "Dad wouldn't do something mean like that. We get to choose where we want to live when we're fourteen, don't we?"

Mrs. Bayley stiffened. Daniel could see that he had hit home. Though Daniel didn't know all the details of his parents' divorce, he did remember the day he sat down in the somber, book-filled office with his parents and their lawyers and the judge. He had secretly hoped to the last minute that his parents would somehow get back together again. But his hopes were completely broken when the judge, an older man, told Daniel and Denise about their visitation rights and custody. Part of the agreement was that when Daniel was fourteen, he could choose to live with his father if he wanted. Ever since that day, Daniel had felt like he was in the middle, being pulled in opposite directions. His parents seemed like two dogs fighting over the same bone. He didn't think any of it was fair.

"Are you trying to blackmail me, young man?" Mrs. Bayley asked, her chin quivering. Daniel could tell that she was suddenly about to cry again. Her eyes were wet. Daniel felt the waves of bad feeling coming down over him like a hot dark blanket.

"Well, you're trying to get rid of my bike," Daniel said, his own voice cracking with emotion. "That's not fair."

"All I want is what's best for you," Mrs. Bayley said, wiping her eyes. "You used to be so popular and happy. That's all I want for you."

"What about the Kramar kids?" Daniel asked.

"I want you to give Barry and his friends a chance first, Daniel," his mother replied, sniffling. "You could just join their club and see what it's like. Bend a little, for my sake, Daniel."

Daniel couldn't bear looking at his mother's pitiful face anymore. He knew she would cry any second. "Ok, I'll try to be friends with those guys," Daniel said with a sigh. Daniel felt desperate to get the ugly bad feeling off himself. "Maybe I could ride the Super Wings every other day, too."

"I'm just afraid everyone will see you as some sort of oddball, riding that old junky bike," Mrs. Bayley said quickly. "You're already self-conscious about your limp, but what's done is done. I'd think you'd try to help your image about things you *could change.* The Super Wings is really a nice bike, and I'm sure you'll fit in much better with the other children with that bike than that old junky Spirit Flyer. Don't you agree?"

"I suppose," Daniel said. He knew what his mother was talking about. Where he used to live, several kids had said mean things about the Spirit Flyer. And the remarks had hurt too. Daniel sighed with confusion. Life seemed so hard. Mrs. Bayley wiped her eyes and patted Daniel on the back. She seemed back to her normal self and Daniel felt grateful.

"I know you won't disappoint me," his mother said. "Now I've got to go to the office. Be nice to Mrs. Jenkins. I'm off."

The Cobra Club was in session again in the Smedlowe's garage at the same time, and the boys were arguing. Barry had called the meeting again because he had failed to convince the club on Saturday night to ask Daniel to join the club.

"But he's a gimp," Alvin protested. "He's probably a real idiot besides."

"No, he's not," Barry said. "I heard my father talking to my mother, and he's a real whiz kid. My dad sees their grades and records and he knows. He'll be in the gifted classes for sure, my Dad said. He said Daniel's record is really special."

"Then he's probably one of those know-it-all guys," Doug said. "Samantha Perkins is in that gifted group, and she thinks she's so hot. And she's just in the third grade."

"You're just jealous because she can read better than you," Barry said.

"*Anybody* can read better than Doug," Freddie said and giggled. "He's in the low group."

"I am not!" Doug said. "I got out of that group last April."

"Did your parents bribe the teacher?" Freddie asked.

"You better shut your mouth, or I'll shut it for you," Doug said. He stood up with his hands in fists. He turned toward Freddie.

"Cool off," Barry said. "We're not talking about Doug. We're talking about Daniel. I say he's club material, and I want to ask him to join."

"But why?" Alvin asked. Alvin was a short boy with a rather big nose. The other boys sometimes called him Nose. Alvin didn't like it, but he never complained too much because he didn't want to be kicked out of the club.

"I just think he's club material, that's all," Barry said. "Besides, he's got a Goliath Super Wings bicycle. That must mean he's ok. Those are supposed to be really great bikes. Mrs. Happy told me about them. She also said it would be good for us if we let him join."

"How would it be good for us?" Doug grunted.

"She just said it would be a lot of points in our favor if we can 'turn him,' as she put it," Barry said. "I don't know what all she meant, but she's an important lady in this town, and I think we need to listen to her. Besides, he can afford the new higher dues the Cobra Club is charging."

"What higher dues?" Doug asked. "No one ever said anything about higher dues to me."

"Or me either," replied Freddie.

"Relax," Barry said with a big smile. "You guys are *charter* members. But from now on, we'll be charging twice the original dues, maybe even three times. We'll all benefit. The club can be in two levels, officers and members, sort of like an army. We'll be the officers, and anyone from here on out will just be the members. But they'll pay higher-priced dues. That's the new rules." The other boys thought for a moment, and then began to grin and nod at one another. Barry smiled.

"I second the motion that we ask Daniel Bayley to join the club," Doug said.

"Good," Barry said. "Now let's give him a chance."

"You were the one who let him sit in that broken chair," Doug said. The other boys began to giggle. So did Barry.

"Well, we have to act nice anyway," Barry said. Then he smiled as a new idea sprang into the boy's mind. "Even if he is Gimpy the Limpy, we need someone to boss around a little bit. We can make him pass an initiation test to join. Lots of clubs make their members do stuff to prove themselves. It'll be fun."

"But what should we do?" Alvin asked. The boys were quiet for a moment. Then Barry began to grin.

"We can talk about it on the way to his house," Barry said. "Let's go."

The boys all grinned at once, hopped on their bicycles and followed their leader into the street.

Daniel was ready to go exploring. He went down to the garage. The two bikes leaned on their kickstands, side by side. Even though his mother was at work, Daniel could feel her right beside him as if she were a ghost.

"I know you won't disappoint me," he heard her say.

He sighed and reluctantly went over to the Goliath Super Wings and knocked up the kickstand. He felt like a traitor because he didn't ride the old red Spirit Flyer. Yet he would have felt just as bad by picking it instead of the Super Wings. You can only ride one bike at a time, he told himself, angry with frustration.

Daniel opened the small side door and pushed the shiny new bike outside. The morning was already getting hot. He was surprised to see Barry and the other boys pedaling up to his house. Barry stared a long time at the golden Goliath Super Wings bicycle. He licked his lips.

"We came to see you," Barry said with a smile. "I'm sorry about that little prank we played. But I've got some great news. We want you to join the Cobra Club."

"Oh," Daniel said flatly. He wondered if Barry was really sorry. Once again it was as if his mother were standing right behind him. Daniel decided to give the boys a chance.

"Let's go to the clubhouse for the initiation," Barry said. "Maybe you could let me ride that Super Wings sometime too."

Daniel pedaled faster to catch up with Barry. They pedaled down Oak until they came to Tenth Street. As they rounded the corner heading east, Daniel saw the two children approaching on red bicycles.

"It's those Kramars," Barry shouted back at the club. The boys began to laugh and get excited.

"We haven't seen who's chicken in quite a while," Barry said. He stood up on his pedals and aimed straight for Susan Kramar. "Come on!"

The other boys yelled and hooted and followed their leader. Daniel pedaled after them, hoping no one would get hurt. He was twenty feet behind the boys when they roared past Susan and John Kramar, forcing them to a stop at the side of the street. Daniel pedaled up slowly.

"Hi," he said, smiling nervously.

"We were just coming to see you," Susan Kramar said. She stared at Daniel's golden Goliath bicycle. Her face looked unhappy.

"We must have made a mistake about you," John Kramar added. "I didn't know you were a member of the Cobra Club. You didn't tell us you had a Goliath bicycle too."

"But I'm not really a member of their club," Daniel said defensively.

"But you're riding around with them, aren't you?" Susan asked. She smiled at him and seemed confused. "Where's your Spirit Flyer?"

"Well, it's kind of hard to explain," Daniel muttered and coughed. "I've got two bikes and since my mom works for Goliath and all, she likes me to ride the Goliath bike too. You understand, don't you?"

The troubled look on Susan's face cut at John's heart. She stared at the golden Super Wings bicycle and frowned.

"So you're not a member of the Cobra Club?" John Kramar demanded.

"No," Daniel said. He was about to explain the situation when Barry yelled.

"Come on, Danny!" Barry shouted from down the street.

"Do you want to go with us or them?" Susan asked. She stared into his eyes so mysteriously it made Daniel feel funny inside.

"I want to go with you guys," Daniel said honestly.

"Then let's go get your Spirit Flyer," John replied. "We can fly out to my Dad's old workshop. I think we've made an interesting discovery."

"Yeah, there's more danger with Goliath Industries than we first thought," Susan added.

"Hey, Danny, come on!" Barry yelled, again. Before Daniel could say anything else, Barry pedaled down the street and coasted up to the group. The other boys in the club were right behind him. "You don't want to be talking to these chicken Kramars. We need to get to the clubhouse so we can initiate you into the Cobra Club. Everything's ready. We don't have time for these idiots."

"So you are one of them," John Kramar accused. Daniel felt his face turning red. He looked at Susan, but her eyes had suddenly gone cold with disappointment.

"Of course he's with us," Barry grunted. "You don't think he'd hang around a bunch of losers like you guys."

Daniel felt trapped. He looked at Susan helplessly, but she looked down. John Kramar was glaring at Daniel.

"Let's go, John," Susan said softly. She looked up at Daniel and shook her head and began pedaling away.

"I guess we had you figured all wrong," John grunted. He pedaled to catch up with Susan.

The two children pedaled their old red bicycles down the street. Daniel's chest was pounding as he watched them ride away. More than anything he wanted to go after them. But without his own Spirit Flyer bicycle, he knew he didn't belong.

"Come on, Danny," Barry repeated. "It's time you rode with the winners in this town."

Daniel watched the Kramars until they turned the corner and were gone. He sighed and rode after the other boys.

COACH GOOBER

6

Daniel was sworn into the Cobra Club that morning. Fortunately, the swearing-in ceremony only took a few minutes. Barry used a sewing needle to stick Daniel's thumb. Daniel had to let a drop of his blood fall into the flame of a candle and repeat the club oath. The whole thing seemed melodramatic to Daniel, but he went along with it so he could get out of the hot little shack. It wasn't until after he was sworn in that Barry told him he still had to pass an initiation test sometime in the future to be a full member.

Daniel didn't worry about it too much. But he was worried about the test he would face that evening. The first practice of the Goliath Sports League began at five-thirty and Daniel dreaded it.

His mom was pleased Daniel had gotten into the Cobra Club. He didn't tell her he still had to pass an initiation test to be a full member. He knew that she would bug him with questions constantly until he was in the club for good.

Even though he was frustrated with his mother, he was relieved that she was happy. She was easier to get along with when she was happy. He still couldn't shake the feeling that he was selling out somehow. He kept seeing the hurt, confused look on Susan Kramar's face. How could you please everyone, he thought? He wondered what his dad would do in his place. His dad didn't try to please people all the time. That's why his mom said he had no social skills. Yet his dad had a hard time keeping a job too. It seemed that if you were too honest, you had to pay for it, one way or another. Daniel wondered whether his dad was really happy. He wondered about his dad a lot.

Thinking of his dad made Daniel feel bad. He tried to push all those worries out of his mind as he got in the car. He had on his black soccer shoes and shorts. Denise was dressed to play ball too. She had her pretty hair in braids. Her mother had bought her a new and expensive jersey blouse that afternoon for practice.

"You should have combed your hair," Mrs. Bayley said, looking at Daniel in the rearview mirror.

"We're just playing soccer," Daniel protested.

"You still need to look neat," his mother replied. "Remember, this is the first time you'll be meeting many of these children. And this is the first time you'll be meeting your coach."

"I wonder if he'll want me to part my hair on the right or on the left," Daniel said.

"Don't be smart with me," Mrs. Bayley said, looking cross. "You know what I mean. First impressions are big impressions."

Daniel didn't argue. He knew it was useless. He had combed his hair, but it hadn't done much good. His hair had been straight all of his life, but the day he had turned twelve, the trouble had started. His hair had begun to get wavy, and it wouldn't stay in place as easily as it used to when he combed it. His mother said he was entering adolescence and that it was a sign of growing up.

Having bright red hair and a ton of freckles was bad enough, Daniel thought to himself. He had been teased about that all his life and expected it. But now his red hair had to go bananas. He was sure that by the time he was thirteen his hair would be full of not only waves, but even curls. The thought horrified the boy. He had tried combing the waves out, but his hair just seemed to go wild, springing off in all different directions. The only thing that helped was cutting it often and keeping it short. But since his family had been busy with the move the last several weeks, he had forgotten to get it cut.

They pulled into the parking lot by the athletic field. The place was packed. Children in shorts and black soccer shoes were everywhere. So were the parents. The smaller children were holding tightly onto their mothers' hands. Fear was written all over their tiny faces.

Daniel sympathized with their fear. He had seen this same kind of thing where he had lived before. He had felt the same way when he was younger, even before the accident. Perhaps the only thing worse than having to play at sports was not playing. Being stuck on the bench where everyone could see that you weren't chosen to play was one of the worst feelings a kid could have.

But that wasn't the lowest you could go. Daniel knew from experience. Being stuck in a wheelchair could be even worse. If you were on the bench, you were at least on the team. But in the wheelchair you were plain out. The four months Daniel spent in a wheelchair had made him feel as if he almost no longer existed. He had lost most of his friends in that time.

His mother hadn't forgotten that time either. She had moved to a new neighborhood in the city just so Daniel would have a chance to start over in a new school. But the kids at that new school treated him about the same, if not worse, because of his limp. By then it began to dawn on him that he might be considered an outsider all his life.

Sometimes his mother seemed desperate to go back to the way things were before the accident. Just after he got out of the wheelchair, things seemed to fall apart. During that time, Daniel noticed the changes in his father. Somehow the accident had broken something inside. Daniel used to lie in his bed at night and hear his parents arguing in the next room. He used to cover his head with a pillow so tightly that he had trouble breathing. Anything was better than hearing the awful voices of his parents fighting.

Moving to Centerville was more or less the same attempt by his mother to change things back to the way they used to be, Daniel thought. She didn't like his limp any more than the kids in his grade. She was probably just as embarrassed as he was in her own way, he figured. But she was determined he would be as normal as everyone else. Playing in the Goliath Sports League wasn't a game to her, and Daniel could tell by looking at the faces of the other parents that it wasn't a game to them either.

"Mr. Goober is your coach," his mother said. "He's that man over there. And don't worry, Coach Carothers already told him about your little problem."

"Swell," Daniel said and sighed. He looked at Coach Goober. He was a hairy man. He wore white gym shorts and had hairy legs and hairy arms. Hairs even peeked out from the neckline of his white T-shirt. He was somewhat short, but very stocky and muscular. He wore a whistle around his neck.

"I'll introduce you," his mother said. She grabbed Daniel's hand and pulled him along. Daniel's face began to turn red.

"I can walk, Mother," he said, yanking his hand free.

"I know you can walk," she said crossly. But she was all smiles again by the time they had reached the coach.

"Coach Goober, this is my son, Daniel," Mrs. Bayley said. "We're new in town. I'm the personnel manager out at the factory."

Coach Goober frowned, trying to think. Daniel decided by the look on the man's face that thinking didn't come easily to the coach.

"Yeah, I remember now," he said. "The redheaded kid with a bum leg."

Daniel looked at his mother. She was still smiling, but he could see that she wasn't smiling inside at all. Her mouth twitched slightly. Daniel knew that twitch well.

"Well, Daniel has a slight limp," his mother said delicately. "But he's got a lot of spirit, don't you, Dan?"

"Sure," Daniel said flatly.

"And he used to be captain of his old soccer team," Mrs. Bayley said firmly. "He was a chosen on the All-City team too."

"Mother!" Daniel groaned.

"I'm sure Coach Goober wants to know about your experience, Dan," his mother said, almost pinching his arm.

Coach Goober didn't seem to notice Daniel's lack of enthusiasm. Daniel decided he was the kind of person who wouldn't notice much of anything except perhaps big pieces of red meat on a dinner plate or large bottles of beer. His mother noticed, however, and shot Daniel a warning glance.

"We're going to have a lot of fun with these kids," Coach Goober said, rubbing his cheek with his hairy hand. Daniel wondered for an instant if the man had workable thumbs. The coach had a heavy dark stubble on his face that probably needed shaving once an hour. He seemed about four hours overdue. He noticed his mother staring at the coach's face too. And she was worried about my hair being out of place, Daniel thought happily to himself.

"Well, I know you probably want to get started," his mother said. "I'll leave you two to get acquainted. You be good, Daniel."

Coach Goober watched Daniel's mother walking away for what seemed like a long time. "Pretty lady, your mom," the coach said. "Where's your dad?"

"They're divorced," Daniel said.

"Yeah?" the coach asked. "Your mom dating anybody?"

"I don't think so," Daniel said. He was surprised at the coach's questions.

"Is that a fact?" the coach grunted. "Well, I want you to know that it don't mean a thing to me that you're a cripple and all. I want you kids to learn the fundamentals, the basics and play ball."

"I'm not exactly crippled," Daniel began to explain.

"Crippled, lame, bum leg, whatever you want to call it, it don't make no difference to me," Coach Goober said. "I don't hold it against you. I had an old coon dog once who only had three legs. He got his right front paw caught in a steel spring trap and the vet had to take it off, whack! Right at the knee. I still got it in my den, you know, kind of like a rabbit's foot, only bigger. But even with just three legs that dog could run coons, let me tell you. He was the best dog I ever had."

"Could he play soccer too?" Daniel asked.

"Soccer? You mean the dog?" Coach Goober looked puzzled. "How could a dog play soccer?"

"Never mind," Daniel said. He coughed and put his hand up over his mouth. The coach was staring down at him suspiciously. "Maybe I should go warm up."

"Yeah, you do that, Red," the coach said. "The team is meeting over by that goal yonder."

Daniel limped away from the coach and for the first time in a long time, he just didn't care. He turned and saw the coach staring at him. The coach smiled and waved him on.

Barry Smedlowe and Doug Barns and the other boys in the Cobra Club were over practicing by the goal. Barry smiled real big when he saw Daniel.

"Same club, same team," Barry yelled out.

"Yeah," Daniel said, trying to be enthusiastic.

"Here comes the coach," Doug said.

Coach Goober blew his whistle and waved his arms and the boys all gathered around. He was frowning so hard at his clipboard that Daniel wondered if he could read.

The coach finally began spitting out names. Daniel yelled, "Here!" when his name was called. All over the playing fields, children were gathered in groups around their coaches. Off to the sides, the adults were gathered too.

"Sit down in a circle, boys," Coach Goober said. Daniel sat with the others. The grass tickled his legs. Coach Goober looked serious. He looked down at his clipboard and then at the young waiting faces. "First of all, you fourteen boys are now to be known as the Rockets." The boys smiled and began whispering among themselves. The coach tooted his whistle lightly and the whispering stopped. "Boys, let's get something straight right here and now," Coach Goober said. "We are a team and a team is like an army, and I am the general in that army and when this whistle blows, you stop everything and listen up."

"How will we know it's your whistle, Coach?" Barry asked. Other whistles could be heard in the distance.

"Don't be a smart mouth, Smedlowe," Coach Goober said with a frown. "You know what I'm saying."

"Yes, sir," Barry said innocently.

"Now boys, you may think we're out here just to play a simple little game and have a little fun, but we're not," Coach Goober said. He seemed to be reading from the clipboard. He waited in silence, looking at each serious face. He reached down and scratched his hairy knee. "Playing ball is a lot like playing the game of life. There are winners and losers. And who do you want to be?"

"Winners!" the boys yelled in unison. Daniel didn't yell because he was taken by surprise.

"That's right, because everyone loves a winner," the coach said. "Everyone respects a winner, whether it's just a ball game or the game of life itself. In the game of life, there's a saying—survival of the fittest.

Do you know what that means?"

"It means you get the other guy before he gets you," Barry said with a grin.

"Smedlowe's exactly right," Coach Goober said, nodding his head. "As soon as you put on those black shoes and the uniform of the Rockets, everyone is your enemy, unless he's a Rocket. We are playing for keeps, as they say. Now on this team we're going to learn the basics, the fundamentals of a good game of soccer. But that's only about forty per cent of what it takes. Do you know where the other eighty per cent comes from? How about you, Red? Do you know?"

"Actually, forty and eighty per cent add up to one hundred and twenty per cent," Daniel said slowly. "You probably meant to say thirty and seventy per cent or—"

"What are you talking about?" Coach Goober asked, frowning. Then he squinted his eyes together on his heavy forehead so tightly, it looked like he had one big black hairy eyebrow. The other boys began to snicker.

"I'm not here to talk arithmetic," the coach grunted. "The only arithmetic I want to see is winning numbers on the scoreboard. Rocket winning numbers."

The coach looked at each face, trying to see if anyone was still snickering. He glared at Daniel before going on.

"What I was saying before is this," he continued. "The fundamentals of the game are just a small part. The other part is . . . attitude. You boys know what I'm talking about when I say attitude?"

They all quickly nodded their heads. The coach smiled broadly and then reached down to scratch his knee again.

"From now on, all Rocket team members are going to have a winning attitude," the coach said. "That's how you play the game of soccer and that's how you play the game of life. If you haven't got a winning attitude, you've got a losing attitude. Is that clear? This town, this state, this whole country has lost its winning attitude over the years, if you ask me. Sure times are hard. Some people say we might be heading for a war. Some even say we're already on the way out, losers. But as my old coach told me, when the going gets tough, the tough get going and bang some heads! Of course, we were playing football then, a real game. But it doesn't matter what the game is, it's attitude, boys, that's what I'm talking about. When you get on that field, it's time for battle. If that other player isn't a Rocket, he's your enemy. And only winners survive."

Coach Goober looked down at his clipboard once more. He read something, squinting his eyes tightly together.

"I have an announcement before we hit the field," he said. "There's some new kind of scoreboard down at the Happy Toy Store, supplied courtesy of Goliath Industries which is also sponsoring this league. It says here, when you get a chance, go by and get a free toy and check out your statistics, whatever that means. Now let's go learn some fundamentals. And remember, Rockets are winners!"

The boys all got up and yelled and ran for the field. Daniel got up slowly, watching his teammates heading for glory. As he turned to go, the coach called him.

"Hey, Red," the coach said. He was frowning.

"Yes?" Daniel asked.

"When I ask you a question, I don't want no smart mouth. Understand me?" Coach Goober asked. He leaned down so close to Daniel's face that Daniel could smell his breath. The coach was a smoker, Daniel could tell.

"I wasn't trying to be a smart mouth," Daniel replied.

"Well, just see that you're not," Coach Goober said suspiciously. "We play by my rules on this team. You got that?"

"Sure," Daniel said simply.

"Good," the coach said. "Now get out and show me what you can do."

Daniel ran toward the others who were already kicking the ball around. The coach watched him limping. The big man spat on the ground and then walked toward the boys, blowing his whistle.

THE
BIG
BOARD
· · · · · · · ·
7

Daniel woke up the next morning feeling
as if he had been stomped on by an elephant all night long. His legs
hurt, his chest hurt, his head hurt. The only thing that didn't hurt was
his hair, and he wasn't sure about that.

He dressed and limped down to the breakfast table slowly. Denise
was already eating. His mother was reading a newspaper and drinking
coffee.

"You look awful," she said when she saw him. "Didn't you sleep
well?"

"It's just from practice," Daniel said wearily. "Those guys think they're
out there fighting World War 3. And Coach Goober loved it. I wonder
who let that gorilla out of his cage."

"Don't call your coach names," Mrs. Bayley said. "That's disrespectful."

"The other guys were calling him Goober the Gorilla, not me," Daniel grunted. "I was too busy getting up off the ground. I don't think half the team has ever played soccer before in their lives. I thought they would kick my kneecaps off. And that was only practice. I'd hate to see what will happen in a real game."

"Oh, don't be a spoilsport," his mother said, turning the page of the newspaper. "You're just a little out of shape."

"I know, and they put me out of shape," Daniel said. He poured cold cereal into a bowl. Then he poured on the milk. "I'm glad this is not a real league season. I don't know if I'll even be able to survive a month with these guys."

"Your first game is Friday," his mother said.

"Our first game is Saturday morning," Denise said cheerfully. "I think we'll win too. I hate our team colors. It's that yucky purple. I wanted to wear my green warm-up jacket, but now it won't look right."

"That's too bad," Mrs. Bayley agreed. "But if you're good, maybe we can get you one that will match your colors."

"Thanks, Mommy, I'd love it," Denise said. She looked at Daniel. "Jimmy Roundhouse's sister is on my team. Jimmy is in your club, isn't he?"

"You like that guy?" Daniel asked. "You don't even know him."

"I think he's cute," Denise said. "Why do you always have to act so snooty about everything? You think you're so smart."

"Daniel is smart," Mrs. Bayley said. She sighed and looked at both of her children. "But you shouldn't act snooty, Daniel. Denise is right."

"I wasn't acting snooty," Daniel complained. "I just said that . . . never mind."

Daniel began eating his cereal again. His sister stuck her tongue out at him and got up from the table. Daniel hurried to finish. He didn't want to have another long conversation with his mother about being a good sport. That had been her lecture topic the night before as they had driven home from practice. She had a lecture for everything, Daniel had decided long ago.

The other boys had made fun of his leg at first, but then the coach had given them his own little talk on sportsmanship. Daniel was embarrassed. The coach had talked about teamwork and how the stronger had to help the weaker and that they were all in it together. Then he had told them about his three-legged coon dog too.

His little lecture had made the other boys keep their comments to themselves. But being yelled at by the coach only made the guys meaner, or so it seemed to Daniel. He had felt like a moving target. More than once he had heard someone mutter, "Get Red," right before they piled up on the ball. And during several pileups, Daniel felt his feet being kicked out from under him. That was the worst time, being on the ground inside the circle of kicking, studded soccer shoes. Daniel was sure he was going to get his teeth knocked out one time, but he jerked his head to the side just in time.

Coach Goober had each boy practice all the positions. Daniel had hoped he could just hide down by the goal net. But the coach wanted each boy to practice being goalie, fullback, halfback and forward. They also had a position called sweeper which was a person who roamed all over the field. Barry Smedlowe had asked to be the sweeper, but the Coach had refused to assign permanent positions. Daniel was embarrassed again when his mother suggested to the coach that Daniel be the goalie. Daniel didn't want to be goalie because he knew you had to be quick and fast. His mother thought you just stood there all the time. But she hadn't gone to a soccer game since he was nine, so he figured she had forgotten.

Coach had talked a lot about the fundamentals of play during the practice. But a lot of the boys didn't even seem clear about the rules. Daniel couldn't believe it. He had yelled out, "Foul!" when he was deliberately kicked, but the coach didn't seem to notice.

"Quit whining," one of the boys on the team had said after Daniel shouted out another foul.

"But those are the rules, you idiot," Daniel replied. He regretted calling the boy an idiot because five minutes later the same boy tripped him, accidentally-on-purpose when they were both going for the ball.

"Stay on your toes!" the coach had yelled at Daniel. And on it went. By the time the practice was over, Daniel had decided the first fundamental of the Rockets was to inflict pain whenever possible. But you couldn't explain that to his mother. Daniel was ready to quit the team and told her so in the car, but she wouldn't hear of it.

"Quit after the first practice?" she had said as if she were surprised. "You have to give them a chance. I'm sure those boys have a few rough edges to wear off. The parents I talked to said they've never had a soccer league in town before. They've had football and baseball but no soccer."

"That doesn't surprise me in the least," Daniel said.

"They may play rough, but they wouldn't hurt you intentionally," his mother had said. "It's only for a few weeks. Besides, you just can't quit. How will it look for me if my own son doesn't participate in Goliath Industries' good-will gesture toward the town?"

Daniel had just nodded and rubbed a sore place on his ribs. He nodded wearily as his mother went into another lecture about the best ways to get along as a new boy in town.

After breakfast, Daniel went to the garage. He stared at the two bicycles for a moment. "Today it's your turn," the boy said softly to the old red bicycle. He knocked the kickstand up and pushed the Spirit Flyer outside. Daniel rode downtown slowly. He purposely rode past the sheriff's office, hoping to see some sign of Susan or John Kramar. He thought it might help if they saw him on the Spirit Flyer. But they didn't appear to be there. He sighed. He figured they probably would never want to speak to him again anyway.

Daniel wasn't sure where he wanted to ride next. He didn't realize how sore he felt until he had ridden a few blocks. When he turned the corner on Main, he saw something that caught his interest. A big tractor-trailer truck was parked in front of the toy store.

Just then, two men appeared from behind the long trailer. They were carrying a long black shiny rectangle. Daniel had never seen anything like it. It appeared to be made of some kind of black plastic or glass. The men had trouble turning the corner into the door of the toy store because the black rectangle was almost twenty feet long and at least seven feet high. Luckily for the men, the old door of the toy store was extra large.

Daniel raced down the street, parked the Spirit Flyer and walked in quickly behind the men. Mrs. Happy had her back turned and didn't seem to notice him. A cold feeling went through Daniel's stomach as the men carried the black object over to a bare wall. The rectangle was about three inches thick. A thin black casing ran around the edge like a frame. The more Daniel looked at the thing, the more uneasy he felt. Suddenly, Daniel had a crazy thought. He decided to hide in the store as long as possible, just to see what was going on.

The men lifted the panel up against the wall. Mrs. Happy directed them to lift one end and lower the other. Then she smiled. "That's it," she said. The men let go. The black panel hung on the wall like a giant picture or mirror. Daniel rubbed his eyes. He hadn't seen any hooks or any wires holding the black panel in place. "Must be a real thin wire or something," Daniel said to himself. The men marched out of the toy store without looking back.

Mrs. Happy walked back to her office and returned with a carpetbag. Daniel was even more surprised to see Barry Smedlowe come out of the woman's office. Barry had a bunch of wrapped candies in his hand. He seemed to be sucking on about four of them at once. "What's that?" Barry mumbled around the candy. He seemed fascinated and puzzled by the long black object.

"Why, that's the Big Board I was telling you about," Mrs. Happy said. "Haven't you ever seen one?"

"No," Barry said. "What does it do?"

"Keep score, silly. What did you think it did?" the old woman grunted and shook her head. "You would think in this day and age, children would know about important things."

The old woman reached in her carpetbag and pulled out a black five-inch cube that seemed to be made of the same black shiny material as the Big Board. Daniel stared as she reached down and pulled a three-pronged plug and wire right out of the top of the cube. He rubbed his eyes and looked again. He was sure the surface where the plug had been was smooth, without any opening.

In the same mysterious fashion, the woman took the plug and pushed it into the bottom edge of the Big Board. A sizzling, electric noise broke the air as the dark panel sparked to life. Lights flashed on and off leaving puffs of blue smoke where the lights had been. The sounds of searing static and electricity crackled throughout the store.

Then it was quiet. The blue smoke lifted and across the top of the Big Board were words written in tiny lights: *The Point System: Official Scores.*

"There we go," Mrs. Happy said, her face beaming with smiles. "Everything appears to be in working order. Of course, it will take some time for the Point System to really get humming along. But once the children all check in with their number cards . . . well, you'll see."

"If it's a scoreboard, what scores does it keep?" Barry asked.

"Goodness me," Mrs. Happy said. "I've never seen such a backward little town as this."

Barry stared at the Big Board and gulped. Except for the words across the top, the rest of the surface was blank darkness. "Well, how does it work?" Barry finally asked. He was afraid Mrs. Happy would call him stupid once again, but she smiled this time.

"Give me your number card, please," she said. "Since you're Number One, you'll be the first child in town to have a rank officially scored by the Big Board." The President of the Cobra Club fished the shiny black card out of his pocket. The old woman grabbed it, turned it over, then quickly stuck it into a slot on the Big Board. Daniel blinked. The slot had just seemed to appear out of nowhere. "Now repeat after me," Mrs. Happy said. "Big Board, Big Board, on the wall, how do I rank in the scores of all?"

"Big Board, Big Board, on the wall, how do I rank in the scores of all?" Barry asked.

In a flash, the Big Board came to life. Rows and columns of numbers appeared out of the dark surface. Then as quickly as it began, it stopped with a ding, like the sound of a cash register opening. New words had appeared in bright purple lights:

****

Barry Smedlow: Level: 1   Rank: 1   Score: 826 Points

****

"See, you're still Number One," Mrs. Happy said. The old woman suddenly stopped. She looked carefully around the room. "I want to show you something else in my office."

Barry followed the old woman back into the room. As soon as they left, Daniel stuck his head back up and stared at the mysterious Big Board. In a flash of purple lights, the Big Board sprang into action. Daniel was horrified when the lights stopped. Four-foot-high letters spelled out the message:

****

Daniel Bayley: We've got your number! You're next!!

****

While Daniel puzzled about what the message meant, he looked back and forth between the Big Board and the old woman's office, suddenly wishing he hadn't been hiding. But something about the mysterious board had a pull on the boy. In fact, that's when Daniel saw an image appear out of the shadowy darkness below the message. Daniel stepped from behind the shelf to get a better look. The image became clearer as Daniel himself walked closer to the dark panel. The moving image inside the Big Board appeared to be a boy that was walking toward the front of the panel. Out of curiosity Daniel walked closer to the Big Board. He was only four feet away when he saw that the boy inside the dark panel was walking with a limp. Then Daniel saw that the boy was also holding a chain. Daniel gasped when the boy limped right up to the front of the panel.

That's when Daniel realized he was looking at a reflection of himself, wavy hair, freckles and all. The boy on the other side smiled, then yanked on the chain. Daniel stumbled forward and yelped at the same time as he fell to the ground. Then Daniel saw a chain going from himself right up into the Big Board.

"It's about time you learned who was boss in this town," the reflection of Daniel whispered. His reflected image began to laugh. "To get along, you have to go along. Got it? The Point System is the only game in town. You've got to play by the rules if you want to be popular again, Gimpy the Limpy!" The reflection laughed again and pulled hard on the chain. Daniel felt a constriction in his throat as the chain pulled tighter.

Then he heard noises coming from Mrs. Happy's office. The big purple letters began glowing on and off rapidly. Daniel scrambled to his feet. He heard the rattling sound of a chain as he ran for the door. His leg seemed to ache horribly as he limped through the aisles of the store. The sound of the chain and cackling laughter followed him all the way outside.

THE ONLY
GAME
IN TOWN
· · · · · · · ·
8

Mrs. Happy and Barry were laughing together as they looked out the front windows of the toy store. They both watched Daniel racing down the street on his bicycle.

"I told you that boy was a snoop, deep down," Mrs. Happy said. Her eyes took on a hard glassy look.

"Boy, he was really scared," Barry said. He popped another little green candy in his mouth. The candies, called Sweet Temptations, came in waxy paper wrappers. "He seemed to be looking at something else on the Big Board. I mean he wasn't just looking at the words."

"He saw more than he bargained for," the old woman said. "But that's what he gets for spying on the Big Board."

"I still can't believe he's got one of those junky Spirit Flyer bicycles and a Goliath Super Wings," Barry said. "How can he have two bicycles?"

"Lots of children have two bicycles," Mrs. Happy replied. "But they can only ride one at a time, correct? So it all depends on which bike he rides."

"But I thought you said there is a danger in those Spirit Flyers," Barry said. "I mean, you've been telling me all summer that you and Goliath Industries work for the secret government behind the government. I thought you said Spirit Flyers were part of a secret invasion here in Centerville?"

"Well, the boy probably doesn't know the dangers of Spirit Flyers," the old woman said. "But he will. Once the Point System gets rolling along, he'll have to decide. You can tell if he's a friend or foe by which bicycle he chooses to ride. Not all those who have Spirit Flyer bicycles use them, fortunately. One of our biggest aims in the government and Goliath Industries is to convince those with Spirit Flyers that their bicycles are inferior and a danger to themselves. Plus when they see what a high-level, fully equipped Goliath Super Wings can do, they'll forget all about those junky Spirit Flyers. It's happened many times, believe me."

"That's another thing," Barry said. "I thought I was supposed to get the first Goliath Super Wings when they arrived."

"Well, I thought you would too since you are Number One and all," the old woman said. "But he moved here with it already in his possession. Not much I could do about that, could I?"

Barry seemed bothered. He had seen firsthand some of the things a Spirit Flyer could do, and he was troubled by their mysterious powers. He didn't trust the old bikes nor did he want one. But he did want a Goliath Super Wings since he had heard so many good things about them from Mrs. Happy.

"Well, when will I get a Super Wings?" Barry complained. "Don't we need them to get rid of those tricky Spirit Flyer bikes?"

"All in good time," Mrs. Happy croaked. She patted the eager boy on the head. "I've made a request to headquarters. Those in authority think that if you help in turning Daniel away from riding his Spirit Flyer, you'll get enough points to qualify for a Super Wings. That's why it was good to get him in your little club of cobras. He needs friends like you to influence him to be reasonable. And once the Point System is rolling along, I think the boy will find it in his best interest to play ball with the rest of us."

"How will the Point System do that?" Barry asked.

"You'll see," the old woman replied with the smile. "This town is about to be blessed with one of our government's finest experimental triumphs. Everyone has to play along with the Point System. It's the only game in town. So let's get set up. I'll need your help since the children will be arriving soon."

The old woman turned away from the window. Barry popped another two candies into his mouth and followed her back into her office.

Daniel rode around aimlessly, thinking hard about what he had seen in the toy store. It took several minutes for his fear to subside. More than anything, he wanted to talk to the Kramar children and ask them questions. But he was afraid they didn't want to talk to him. Daniel figured the image in the Big Board was probably the ghostslave that the Kramar children had mentioned. But the reflection seemed a lot more real and powerful than any old ghost he had ever read about!

Just looking into the eyes of his dark reflection on the Big Board made Daniel feel like he was looking into the deepest, most secret part of himself. There was something scary about seeing that. What was worse was the feeling that the Big Board might show others who you really were deep down.

Daniel rode downtown slowly. He purposely rode past the sheriff's office again. He didn't see any Spirit Flyer bicycles, but what he did see interested the boy. A man in a uniform got out of the side door of a blue van. He pulled himself into a wheelchair and closed the sliding door. Daniel looked both ways and darted across the street on his old red bike for a better look.

The man in the wheelchair smiled as he saw Daniel coming. He appeared to be some kind of policeman.

"Are you the sheriff?" Daniel asked.

"I'm a deputy," the man said. "My name's George. George Baker. What's your name?"

"Daniel Bayley," he said. "I'm new in town."

"I've heard."

"Really?" Daniel asked.

"It's hard to live in a town as small as Centerville and not hear about anyone new moving in," George said. "But in this case, the sheriff's children, Susan and John Kramar, mentioned meeting you. She was speaking mighty highly of you a few days ago. Saturday, I believe it was."

"Oh," Daniel said. A lot had happened since then to change her opinion, but he wasn't sure he wanted to talk about that to this man. Still, George seemed very nice and willing to talk. And Daniel had sympathy for anyone in a wheelchair. "Do you know John and Susan well?"

"Known them all their lives," George said.

"Oh," Daniel said. He looked at the deputy's wheelchair. "I was in a wheelchair once for four months. Me and my dad were hit by a drunk driver."

"That's a shame," George said. "I was in an accident myself. Hurt my back."

"I'm sorry," Daniel said.

"You learn to live with it," the deputy said. "Or you don't."

"I guess I better go," Daniel said. Then he had an idea. "If you see Susan or John, would you tell them things aren't the way they seem? They may or may not understand, but I'd appreciate it."

"I'll tell them," George said. He had an easy smile.

"Thanks," Daniel said. George turned and wheeled up a wooden ramp that was on top of the steps. Daniel pedaled back into the street. When he looked back, the deputy had already disappeared into the office.

Daniel rode back down toward the town square. That's when he noticed several children moving toward Main Street. The children looked excited. When Daniel turned the corner on Main, he saw a bigger commotion. Down the block, in front of Happy Toy Store, all kinds of kids, young and old, short and tall, were gathering in a crowd. The sidewalk was impassable because so many bicycles were parked on it. And the front door of the toy store was jammed.

Every so often, a child clutching a small toy would work his way out through the crowd. Daniel remembered Coach Goober's announcement about the free toys and the scoreboard in the toy store. All the coaches must have made the same announcement. Then it occurred to Daniel that the mysterious Big Board was probably what the coaches were referring to in their announcements.

Daniel rode along with the crowd and parked his Spirit Flyer. He looked through the big front windows of the store and saw Barry Smedlowe handing out toys. Across the store, high on the wall, the Big Board was in motion. Lighted numbers flashed by and then paused. Every so often, a groan or the sound of applause or cheers was heard.

Just then, Daniel noticed Barry Smedlowe waving from inside the store. "Come on in," Barry was saying.

Daniel nodded and inched his way toward the front door. He got a break when a large round boy pushed his way out of the toy store through the crowd. That left an opening as the other kids stood aside. Daniel darted through the door before the crowd closed in once more. A man standing by the door looked at Daniel for a second but then let him pass.

The inside of the store was full of the voices of children. Two men in uniforms were standing behind the long counter with the cash register along with Barry Smedlowe. One man would give Barry the toys. He was putting them into small purple plastic bags. Then he gave the toys to the waiting children, calling out each child's name. The other man, who was holding a clipboard, would make a mark. Daniel assumed they were checking off names.

"This is free," Barry yelled. He tossed a sack to Daniel. He opened the sack and looked inside. The toy appeared not to be much of a toy at all, but a pad of paper, sort of like graph paper. At the top of the page were the words: *Point System Scores.* Another object was in the bag that appeared to be made of rubber. At first, Daniel couldn't tell what it was. Then he realized it was a kind of eraser that you slipped on the end of your pencil.

Across the room, a shout went up as a bell rang. The Big Board was flashing lights and numbers at a dizzying speed. Daniel closed the sack and walked closer. Children were gathered in front of the Big Board, staring up at it as if in a spell. They looked exactly like children often look when watching television. Their mouths were slack and hung open, and a sort of glazed look was in their eyes. Each was holding up his or her black number card.

"My turn, my turn!" they would yell out when the mysterious black panel paused. Then Mrs. Happy would take a number card and instruct the owner how to address the Big Board.

"Big Board, Big Board, on the wall, how do I rank in the scores of all?" a little boy shouted. The Big Board went into action. Lights flashed and numbers danced. Then the words and numbers froze.

****

Timmy Bellows: Level: 1   Rank: 76   Score: 740 Points

****

"My points went up and my rank got better!" the boy named Timmy yelled. The Big Board spit his number card out. "It must have been those practice goals I scored last night. See? I was ranked seventy-eight before I came in here."

Mrs. Happy held her hands up. She smiled on the children. They finally stopped talking. "Now you've all had your turn," the old woman said cheerily. "So it's time to let the others have their chance. Go out the front door quietly." Their faces fell as they turned and walked out with the others.

The old woman looked straight at Daniel. She stared at him for a moment quietly. Barry ran from behind the counter and slapped Daniel on the back. Mrs. Happy smiled.

"It's sort of like a computer," Daniel said, staring at the mysterious dark panel. "And the lights are a kind of digital display."

"This boy knows his stuff, I can tell," Mrs. Happy. "You'll be getting points for that."

"You ought to give the Big Board a try," Barry said eagerly. "Lots of numbers and ranks are changing. It's great. There's never been anything like this in Centerville."

"This is the scoreboard all the coaches were talking about?" Daniel asked.

"You are a perceptive boy," Mrs. Happy said. She walked over to Daniel. She reached out and pinched his cheek cheerfully. "I've heard you were special."

Daniel stared hard at the dark panel. For a moment he thought he saw a blurred image in the deep darkness. He rubbed his eyes and looked again. But the image, if it had been there, was gone. Daniel felt a strange pulling sensation. Without thinking, he drew the little black number card out of his pocket.

"So you want to see how you rank on the Big Board, do you?" the old woman said with a smile.

Daniel shrugged his shoulders. Then he nodded slowly. "I guess I do," he replied.

"Well, like I tell all the other children," the old woman said with a twinkle in her eye, "it's the only game in town."

RANK
BLANK

· · · · · · · ·

9

Daniel waited as a new group of children streamed into the store. They ran to the counter by the cash register. Barry had several purple plastic bags all ready.

"Show me some numbers," Barry called out. "Numbers closest to one go first. Hold up your number cards." Barry went from the lowest to the highest number. He tossed the plastic bags and called out names. Occasionally he had to ask a name since several of the kids had just moved to town. "Now go check out your official rank on the Big Board," Barry said. He pointed toward the wall where the huge black panel seemed to wait in electric excitement. The children walked over obediently.

Daniel joined the crowd, filled with curiosity.

Mrs. Happy stood beneath the Big Board and smiled as the children gathered before her. "It's good to see all my little Centerville friends again," she said sweetly. The children smiled and whispered. She waited as they got quiet. "Now I want you all to listen carefully as I introduce the Big Board."

Daniel moved closer. He had been hearing a humming noise and had decided it was coming from the Big Board. The purple letters at the top glowed in the hum.

"Is that the new scoreboard?" a boy named Bobby asked.

"Yes, the Big Board is a wonderful machine that is very much like a scoreboard," Mrs. Happy said. "It is an expensive gift from Goliath Industries, the company where many of your parents work. This is just one of the products Goliath manufactures. Though it will keep track of scores and statistics for the soccer league, it is much more than a regular scoreboard. As my friend Daniel Bayley said just a few minutes ago, the Big Board is something like a computer."

The other children looked over at Daniel with respect. Daniel felt embarrassed by all the attention and looked down. Some of the children whispered. Then they looked up at the mysterious dark panel with wonder in their eyes.

"Let me explain," Mrs. Happy said. "The Big Board keeps the Official Scores, but not only the scores and statistics of the sports league. It keeps all the scores and statistics of all kinds of points. That's what makes it so wonderful. And what makes it even better is that it's up to the date, to the very second, adding and subtracting points."

"What do you mean by points?" Bobby Tipton asked.

"Let me try to give you an example," the old woman said. "How many of you have seen a beauty pageant on television?" Daniel raised his hand. All the other children in the room had their hands raised too. "In the contests on TV, each person is scored points for certain qualities, like appearance, talents, best personality, most popular and so forth,"

Mrs. Happy paused to make sure the children were listening. "The judges record all these qualities as points. The person with the most points wins the contest. The Point System is just like that, only it covers more things than a beauty contest. In fact, it covers everything and makes it all *Official!* All your good points and bad points are added up by the Big Board. Then you can see your overall score and ranking among the other children. We call that the Big Picture."

The old woman paused again. Daniel began to listen more carefully. "For example, everyone knows who's the most popular girl and boy at school," Mrs. Happy said. "Sometimes there's even a vote taken for a yearbook. Well, with the Big Board, you get credit for those popularity points. They become Official and show up in your total score on the Big Board. Now how would you like that?"

"Popularity points?" a girl named Cindy Meyers asked. Then she smiled. She knew she was one of the most popular girls in the seventh grade because she was head cheerleader for the junior varsity teams. She was also very pretty and had beautiful blond hair. "I think keeping track of popularity points is a great idea."

"But it's not just popularity points or scores from the soccer games," Mrs. Happy said. "Every day you are either adding or subtracting points by the way you act and perform. Even a game of one-on-one basketball can give you credit on the Big Board. It's all added into your personal score. Popularity points, score points, the points you get at school on your papers and report cards."

"Grade point averages are added in?" Daniel asked. He looked up at the mysterious Big Board with more interest.

"Not only the overall grade point average but even points on the papers themselves," the old woman replied eagerly. "All your school-work and records are taken in by the Big Board. Of course, you aren't in school right now, but if you got a ninety-eight on a math quiz, the Big Board would add that into your overall point total."

"You mean you get ninety-eight points for a math quiz?" Jeff asked.

He looked worried. He wasn't good at math. "But in soccer games you only get one point if you score a goal."

"Don't be worried," Mrs. Happy said with a reassuring smile. "You know it's not the same thing and so does the Big Board. That's the exciting thing about the way the Point System works. It puts things into perspective in the Big Picture. It's like all the points of all the games are added up fairly. A math quiz isn't the same as a big test and a practice game isn't as important as the Super Bowl. Some things are more important than others. The Big Board knows what's important in this town, and it gives you the exact credit you deserve. That's the wonder of it."

"I do like the idea of popularity points," Cindy Meyers said, running her hand through her long blond hair.

"It's popularity points, good points, bad points, grade points, scores of game points, status points, statistic points, I.Q. points, personality points, beauty points, handsome points, brownie points, age points, friendly points, unfriendly points, snobbish points, credits, mistakes, money points, the value points of things you own (which is almost the same as money points). If it's part of who you are, then you can count on it going somewhere into the Big Board," Mrs. Happy said. The children hung on her words as they began to understand. "In fact, everything you do and everything you have and everything you are, goes into the Big Board in the form of points."

"Wow," Jeff whispered.

"Wow, indeed," said the old woman. "It's like a big game to find where you add up in the Big Picture of Centerville. All the points and their level of importance and value go into the Big Board and out comes your personal score. And if you really want to know, you can get a Point Breakdown sheet to see your strong and weak areas. Or you can compare your score with the scores of your friends."

Daniel frowned as he tried to understand what the old woman was saying. He certainly knew what popularity points were, though they had never been Official, as she had said. Every kid knew who the popular kids were. Or beauty points. "You mean each person is like a collection of all their points?" Daniel asked. "They all add up to make you?"

"Now there's a smart boy," Mrs. Happy said.

"So you can be bad in school work, for example, and lose points, but if you play well in a soccer game, then it sort of makes up for it in another way?"

"You are a bright boy," Mrs. Happy said with a smile. "That's it exactly. That's the way the game works. And that's the way things in life work, only this is a scientific way to put it all into perspective."

"That's just common sense when you think about it," Jeff said to the children around him. Even though he was bad in math and spelling, it was his good athletic ability that mattered to his friends. "Every one's got their good points, and they kind of make up for their bad points. It's sort of like a big report card, only for all sorts of things."

"See, I knew you children knew what the Point System was," the old woman said. "It's like a game played in every town all over the world. In fact, it's the only game in town and in the whole world, really. It's performance that counts. Each person gets the points he or she deserves. And the Big Board is just there as a community service to count those points."

"And the Big Board can add all the points up fairly?" Cindy Meyers asked with concern. Her mother had often scolded her for not doing well in her schoolwork because she spent too much time practicing her cheerleading. Cindy felt she had to practice to be good. But her mother never quite saw it that way.

"When you're a winner, it shows up on your score in the Big Board," Mrs. Happy said enthusiastically. "A pretty head cheerleader like you should get the credit she deserves, don't you think?"

"Yes, I worked hard on my cheers," Cindy agreed. Then she realized the old woman almost seemed to have read her mind. Was that possible, the girl wondered?

"So who wants to be first?" the old woman asked. "I need someone to volunteer their number card."

Jeff shot up his hand quickly. He stepped in front of the crowd, clutching the black plastic card. Number three hundred and twelve was stamped on the card.

"The way the Big Board operates is fairly simple," the old woman said. "Just put your card in this slot. Remember the rank number you had on the card. It may change." She took Jeff's hand and guided the card toward the Big Board. Daniel watched carefully as a slot opened up. The Big Board hummed louder as the card went in. "Now repeat after me," Mrs. Happy said. "Big Board, Big Board, on the wall, how do I rank in the scores of all?"

"Big Board, Big Board, on the wall, how do I rank in the scores of all?" Jeff said softly. The Big Board whirred with numbers and flashing lights. The children stepped back in fear and surprise at the commotion. Then the lights froze with the information.

****

Jeff Fenly: Level: 1   Rank: 135   Score: 555 points

****

Mrs. Happy pulled the card out. She handed it to Jeff.

"You must be quite a soccer player, young man," she said. "Look at the improvement in your rank. You were number three hundred and twelve and now you are all the way up to one hundred thirty-five. That's an enormous climb for such a young boy like you."

Jeff smiled and beamed. A few of his friends patted him on the back. But some of the other children weren't as happy for Jeff. They looked down at the numbers of their cards and then looked up eagerly at the Big Board. Daniel looked at his number card too.

"Me next," Bobby Tipton said. He stepped forward holding up his card which had the number thirty-seven. Mrs. Happy told him what to say and he listened carefully. Then she helped press the number card into a slot in the black panel.

"Big Board, Big Board, on the wall, how do I rank in the scores of all?"

The Big Board flashed into action. Daniel watched as the numbers lit up on the screen. Then it froze with the information.

****

Bobby Tipton: Level: 1   Rank: 175   Score: 433 points

****

Mrs. Happy pulled the number card out of the Big Board and handed it back to Bobby. The number on the card was now one hundred seventy-five, matching the rank on the Big Board. He stared at the card and frowned. Then he looked up at the Big Board. Then he looked back down at the card.

"My rank got worse," Bobby said.

"That's a shame," Mrs. Happy said. "You win a few points. You lose a few. But that's the way the game is played, isn't it?"

All the children looked at little Bobby. He seemed confused by the whole thing. Daniel looked at the Big Board with new respect. "There are only so many children in town so there are only so many ranks," Daniel said slowly. "So if Jeff gets a better rank, that means he replaces whoever else was in that spot before him."

"You are a smart boy," Mrs. Happy said.

"In other words, there can't be two number thirty-threes," Daniel said.

"Of course not," the old woman replied. "That's not the way the game is played. When you slice a pie, there are only so many pieces to give out, don't you agree?"

"Well, I'm going to get what's coming to me," Cindy Meyers said. She pushed her way to the front of the crowd and gave Mrs. Happy her number card. The other children quickly crowded around Mrs. Happy, all trying to take their turns to see how they fit in the Big Picture of Centerville.

Daniel stood back and watched as the Big Board flashed out the scores and rankings. About half the children went up in points and rank while the others lost points and were ranked farther away from number one. Finally, Daniel was the only one left who hadn't taken a turn. Mrs. Happy looked over at him and smiled.

"Ready to see how you stack up against your friends?" Mrs. Happy asked.

"Yeah, give it a try," Barry Smedlowe said as he stepped up behind Daniel. Barry held up his number card. "And since we're talking about ranks, I want everyone to know who is Number One in this town."

Barry smiled broadly as the other children stared with envy at the single digit on his number card.

"How did you get to be Number One?" Cindy asked. She didn't really like Barry and couldn't see how he could possibly be ranked above her, let alone be Number One.

"Yeah," Jeff added. "When we first got these cards back in July, that was just a drawing for those free toys. It was just chance."

"That's the way the game is started," Mrs. Happy said. "But the game of life is often left up to chance, isn't it?"

"Yeah, that's just the way the cookie crumbles," Barry sneered, but then quickly smiled. He had been trying to change his image all summer so the other children would like him. "Take your turn, Daniel."

Daniel sighed. He looked down at his number card and the shadowy image of his face. Five hundred and seventy-two was stamped in gold on the black card. With a shaking hand, he put the card into the slot on the mysterious black panel. "Big Board, Big Board, on the wall, how do I rank in the scores of all?"

The Big Board whirred into life with lights and numbers flashing. But this time it seemed to go on longer before finally coming to a halt. Daniel stared at the information in surprise.

****

Daniel Bayley:*** Level: ?   Rank: ?   Score: ?

****

"Why doesn't he have any rank or anything?" Barry asked.

Mrs. Happy frowned, then looked at Daniel. "That's because of those three stars by his name," she said seriously. "Those stars are called asterisks. Do you know what they mean?"

"No," Daniel said.

"Trouble," Mrs. Happy said. "Something in your file is withholding your rank. And without a rank number, you might as well not even be in the game."

"What trouble?" Daniel asked anxiously.

"Let's check it," Mrs. Happy said. "Big Board, Big Board, a rank is not seen. Tell us what these stars can mean."

The Big Board whirred into life. The numbers and lights flashed a little longer this time. Then an explanation shot across the screen.

****

Daniel Bayley: RANK BLANK. Point Breakdown: Possessions: Two bicycles: Super Wings and Spirit Flyer. The owner must choose one bike. RANK BLANK until problem eliminated!

****

Daniel blinked in surprise. A cold feeling suddenly formed a knot in his stomach. As he looked around, he noticed no one was moving, as if they were frozen in time. But Mrs. Happy was looking at him. Her eyes almost seemed to glow red.

"The Big Board is protecting you from further embarrassment," the old woman said in a whisper. "The others can't see what we see. But you know what's holding you down. I know your mother recognizes this problem. And I would think a smart boy like you would see that Spirit Flyers are bad for you and this community. To get along, you've got to go along. Time is running out."

The old woman stared at Daniel so hard that he became uncomfortable. He felt as if she was looking right inside him. She snapped her fingers. The children seemed to wake up and move again. Only four words were left blinking on and off on the Big Board.

****

Daniel Bayley: Rank Blank.

****

"Rank Blank . . ." the children whispered and looked at Daniel as if he were some kind of oddity.

Daniel took his number card. There was nothing but blank darkness where the number had been. The other children began to whisper. Some began to laugh. Then there was more laughter.

"Rank Blank, Rank Blank, Rank Blank, Rank Blank," the children chanted as Daniel's face turned red. Then they laughed again. They were still laughing as Daniel ran from the store.

SUMMER
PARTY
PLANS
· · · · · · · ·

10

In just four short days the Big Board had become the new sensation of Centerville. By that time, all the children with number cards had visited Happy Toy Store and taken a turn with the Big Board. Ranks went up and ranks went down as the Point System got rolling along.

Deep down, everyone knew what the Point System was immediately. They had always known. The children already knew who was popular and who was good at what from years of being in the same school together. They also knew who was unpopular and who didn't play games well. They knew who did poorly at things like arithmetic and so forth.

But having an Official Score of those things put it all in a new light. Seeing your name and the number of your rank and point total in bright purple letters on the Big Board changed everything. Most kids began keeping track of their scores on the little pads of Point System graph paper. No one quite understood how the Big Board worked, but they could count. It didn't take a genius to know that number seventy-six was behind number seventy-five and in front of seventy-seven.

The children began to talk in new ways about where they "stacked up in the Big Picture of Centerville." And since a person's point total and rank could change from day to day, and even hour to hour, it became important to check in often with the Big Board on how you were doing. They quickly learned that a good practice on their soccer team could mean extra points. And in the same way, a poor performance during practice could mean points lost, perhaps even a rank number.

Happy Toy Store was a busy place as the children streamed in to see if their point total and rank had gone up or down. And since there couldn't be two persons with the same rank number, you never quite knew where you stood in the Big Picture for very long. Though it was often confusing, the children soon learned not to complain. It became common knowledge that if you complained very much, you were acting like a poor sport which lost you points. The children who wanted to get points ahead kept their mouths shut and played along.

On Friday evening, the Rockets' first game was against the Blasters. The game took on new importance because of the Point System. Daniel crowded up around Coach Goober with the rest of the boys as the coach read off positions from his clipboard. Daniel was both disappointed and relieved to be placed on the bench with two others, Marvin and Richard. All the Cobra Club members except him were playing first string. The starting players cheered and ran to the field to take their positions. Coach Goober stood outside the sidelines, yelling instructions. The game began.

"I just knew it," Marvin said with great disappointment as he sat down

on the bench next to Daniel. "I'll never get out of the bottom hundred on the Big Board if I don't get a chance to get in there and prove myself."

"You'll get a chance, Marvin," Coach Goober said over his shoulder. "All you boys will get a chance to prove yourselves. Even you, Red."

"But he's Rank Blank," Richard said with disgust. Daniel just sighed and acted like the label didn't embarrass him. But deep down, it did, of course. Talk got around quickly in Centerville. Almost everyone knew that the Big Board had erased his number from the number card, though they didn't know the reason why, which made them even more suspicious of the newcomer. As far as Daniel knew, he was the only Rank Blank person in town.

Daniel looked across the field. Two other games were going on in different fields. Parents were lined up along the borders, either cheering or yelling at the referees. Daniel knew his mother was somewhere in the line of parents off to his left, waiting for him to play. He didn't look to find her, however. Instead, he thought of the Big Board and how quickly the Point System had taken over the town.

For the first two days, using the Big Board had been free. But on the third day, Mrs. Happy had begun charging a quarter for each turn. In fact, there was a slot on the Big Board where you put your money, just like on a soda machine. No one had noticed it before the third day. It just seemed to appear.

All the talk of the Point System and the Big Board seemed somewhat bizarre to Daniel. Yet he could understand the other kids' concern about their rank. Everyone wanted to be popular and accepted. No one wanted to be in the lower ranks of the Point System. No one wanted to be known as a loser or a bad performer.

But there were other rewards than just having a good rank in the Point System. Before the games began that evening, a man from Goliath Industries had made an announcement. Those children who ranked in the top two hundred on October 1 would receive a free one-year membership for their whole family at the new Goliath Country Club. The club was scheduled to be opened by then. The children that were on the first place team, the Superstar team, at the end of August would also get the same privileges in advance and some free prizes and money too. The promise of such prizes made the Big Board even more important. Being high up not only meant you were popular, but it was like adding cash to your pocket.

Daniel had avoided the Big Board and the toy store as much as possible that week. But he couldn't avoid the Point System. He was already something of an outsider as a new kid in town, and as a boy with a limp. But being known as Rank Blank, as the Big Board put it, made him even more of an oddball to the other kids. His mother had been very upset when she found out that he was without a number. Denise had already worked her way into the Top Hundred by Friday morning, checking in at number seventy-six.

His mother seemed to think he was Rank Blank because he was just a new boy and something of a loner. She also feared that it was because of his limp, though she didn't say anything about it to Daniel. She hoped that once the other children got to know him, he would fit into the Point System like the others.

"It's performance that counts," his mother had told Daniel when she first heard that he was Rank Blank. "I've been trying to tell you that all along, just like I tried to tell your father. I hope you wise up to the way things work in the world. It's just common sense."

Daniel hadn't argued. Neither did he tell her what the Big Board and Mrs. Happy had said about the problem. He knew that if his mother found out it involved the Spirit Flyer that she would try to make him get rid of the old bicycle. So to play it safe he had ridden the Spirit Flyer less and less. He had also stopped talking about the old bicycle so much around his mother. He talked instead about the team and the Cobra Club. By the end of the week he was almost glad he was a member of the Rockets and the Cobra Club. At least he felt a part of something even though he was Rank Blank. Daniel was beginning to think his mother had a point about being involved with the other kids. He wondered if she had been right all along.

Daniel still couldn't understand why the Big Board disqualified him because of his Spirit Flyer. Though he remembered the warnings of the Kramar children about Goliath Industries and an attack on the town, he didn't see how it all fit together. Deep down, he began to wonder if their fears about Goliath Industries and Mrs. Happy were correct. He hadn't seen either Susan or John for days. They weren't on any of the soccer teams. They seemed to have dropped out of sight.

The boy was so deep in his thoughts that he didn't see the Rockets score the first goal. The cheering team members woke him up from his daydream. The parents on the sidelines were cheering louder than the boys. There was a pause in the play as both coaches sent in substitute players.

"Bayley, get in there at left fullback," Coach Goober barked at Daniel. "Tell Alvin to come out."

Daniel nodded and ran onto the field. He was determined not to think about his limp.

"Why do I have to get replaced by a Rank Blank cripple like you?" Alvin muttered. "I was just getting warmed up."

Daniel played out the half. He didn't make any spectacular plays, nor did he make any mistakes. In fact, he only engaged in play about four times. An opposing player kicked him once hard in the shins and Daniel fell. But the referee missed it. The Rockets scored two more times. As Daniel clomped off the field at the half, he looked over at his mother briefly. She smiled, but Daniel could tell she wasn't really happy.

During the short half-time break, the other boys discussed strategy with the coach and drank water. Daniel sipped water from a paper cup, listening.

"That goal I scored will be worth twenty points on the Big Board, I bet," Barry Smedlowe said proudly. "Maybe even more. Too bad I can't be ranked higher than Number One."

"Well, I could have been improving my score if I hadn't got benched," Alvin said. "I don't know why the coach put ol' Blanky in to play instead of me."

The other boys laughed. Coach Goober came over with the clipboard. He frowned as he looked at it.

"Ok, listen up," the coach barked out. "The starting team goes back in. I want to see some hustle out there. You boys were looking awful tired toward the end of the half. Remember, it's survival of the fittest. Do you want to be the Superstar team or not?"

The boys yelled as they ran back out on the field. Daniel felt comfortably invisible on the bench. He sighed as he retied his shoes. He wondered if the game performance would really change the scores on the Big Board as much as the other boys hoped.

Rank numbers seemed to have settled, more or less, among the children by that Friday. The big, sudden changes were less frequent, Daniel had noticed, as he watched the kids compare their number cards and Point System graph sheets. Barry Smedlowe and the Cobra Club were still locked in at numbers one through seven. Most of the children couldn't understand why since Barry had never been very popular before. In fact, he was disliked by a lot of the other children in town. He was seen as a bully. The older kids didn't trust him because he was the school principal's son. They thought he got special favors. Some thought that his father had pulled some strings somehow to get him ranked Number One.

But Barry knew a few things the other children didn't know. That Friday morning, he had let at least one secret out. There was a small screen, something like a TV screen on the Goliath Combo-Gizmos toys. Thanks to Mrs. Happy's help, Barry had figured out that the odd little toy worked something like a radio receiver. The Combo-Gizmo could apparently receive signals from the Big Board. If you stuck a number card in the right slot, the little screen could tell the accurate ranking of whoever's number card was in the slot. The Combo-Gizmo couldn't do all the other things the Big Board did, but even so, everyone realized right away how valuable the little Combo-Gizmos could be. And Barry owned every Combo-Gizmo in town, except the one that belonged to Daniel. But since Daniel was Rank Blank, his Combo-Gizmo wouldn't work properly.

The toy store, strangely enough, was out of stock of the suddenly popular toy. The kids who had sold their Combo-Gizmos to Barry were more than a little angry. All day Friday they had tried to buy them back. Some children had offered up to three times their regular price, but Barry had refused to sell, realizing a good thing when he saw it. He gave the ex-owners one free turn to show them he was a nice guy. After that, he charged fifteen cents a try, which was cheaper than what Mrs. Happy charged. And already, before the game that evening, Barry had made over three dollars from anxious children who wanted a before-game and after-game point total.

Barry's business with the Combo-Gizmos gave him new status points among the kids, even if they were envious. Those new points quickly showed up on the Big Board. He had been gloating all day. The other children had begun to see him differently as his point total rose.

The Rockets beat the Blasters, six to two. Daniel played only a short time in the second half. When he missed an easy ball tackle on a player who then scored, Coach Goober put Daniel back on the bench.

"Why didn't you take that ball away?" Coach Goober yelled as Daniel limped off the field.

"I tried," Daniel said defensively, though he knew he hadn't really tried as hard as he could have.

"You're benched for the rest of the game," Coach Goober muttered. "No wonder you're Rank Blank."

After the Rockets won and shook hands with the opposing team, the coach invited all the boys to go get ice cream at Sammy's Fast Food Place, which was located off the four-lane highway just outside of Centerville. Daniel didn't really want to go, but his mother insisted.

The Cobra Club boys all sat together at the same table inside the tiny restaurant. While the boys licked their drippy vanilla cones, Barry told them about his new plan. "I'm going to invite all the kids who rank in the top two hundred to come to a giant party at my house," Barry said. He stuck the rest of the cone in his mouth and chewed it up. "I'm calling it the Super Summer Party."

"When are you going to have it?" Doug asked excitedly.

"The same night as the End of Summer Town Pool Party," Barry said proudly. "Mrs. Happy is letting me put up a poster in the toy store, right by the Big Board."

The End of Summer Town Pool Party was a tradition in Centerville. It took place on the last Saturday in August. Most of the children and families in town went to swim and eat. The admission price was donated to good causes, like books for the library and playground equipment at the town park where the pool was located.

"Two hundred kids is a lot of kids," Doug Barns said. "Besides, I've heard a lot of kids are going to the Top Hundred Party at the town pool party. They reserved the clubhouse. In fact, Cindy Meyers and Craig Banks have invited me. He's worked his way to number eight and she's number nine."

"Well, they didn't invite me on purpose, and I'm Number One," Barry snarled. "That's one reason I decided to have my own Super Summer Party, to show those snobs who's who in this town. They made a big mistake when they didn't invite Number One, and they need to be taught a lesson. In fact, I don't think I'll invite Cindy or Craig. And without an invitation to my party, I bet their point total will drop."

"But how do you know the other kids will come to your party?" Jimmy asked. "I mean, a lot of kids are still pretty mad at you for buying up all the Combo-Gizmos and other stuff. I heard some . . . , well, you know I don't say those kind of things about you."

"You better not," Barry warned, slapping his fist in his hand.

"Jimmy's got a point, though," Alvin said. "How do you know you'll get the kids to come to your party and not Craig and Cindy's party?"

"Because I'm making some new plans," Barry said with a sneaky smile. "I'm not Number One in this town for nothing."

The other boys laughed knowing that Barry must be up to one of his old tricks. They licked their cones and smiled.

"By the way, you're invited to my party too, Red," Barry said to Daniel. "Even though you're Rank Blank. But you won't be without a number for long. That's all part of my whole plan. After you pass your initiation test, you'll be up on the Big Board with the rest of us."

"How do you know that?" Daniel asked. He was suddenly interested.

"I've been talking to Mrs. Happy about it," Barry said with a grin. "Being Number One puts me on the inside track in this town. Just trust me. With my help, you'll be ranking right up there in the Point System with the rest of us before you know it. You can count on it."

Daniel finished his ice cream cone, wondering what Barry meant. The thought of not being Rank Blank did appeal to the boy. But at the same time, he wondered how that could be arranged since he owned a Spirit Flyer. As the other boys laughed and joked, Daniel wasn't sure he wanted to find out.

FIRE
AND
SMOKE
• • • • • • • • •

11

Not everyone was happy about the Big Board and the recent changes it had made in the town. Several parents had complained about it. They didn't see how such a system could be fair. Those parents whose children ranked the lowest on the Big Board were especially upset.

The next day, on Saturday evening, five days after the Point System had been in operation, a group of parents decided to take action. They went to the toy store to share their feelings with Mrs. Happy. Sheriff Kramar was in uniform as he walked through the front door, followed by a committee of parents.

"Good afternoon, Sheriff," Mrs. Happy said with a twinkle in her eye.

"I'm just about to close up."

"Mrs. Happy, we've come as a kind of committee or delegation, you might say, to speak to you about the Big Board," Sheriff Kramar began. He coughed and looked uncomfortable. The other parents introduced themselves quickly.

"Is there some sort of problem?" Mrs. Happy asked.

"Well, yes there is," Sheriff Kramar said. "A lot of us feel that this Point System way of ranking children is bad for the kids. I've had complaints about name calling and now number calling, as they put it. Low numbers."

"It's just awful," a woman blurted out. Her name was Mrs. Hubert. "My little Nicolas is having a terrible time with his friends. They just tease him until he cries."

"What's Nicolas's rank?" the old woman asked.

"Five hundred sixty-four," Mrs. Hubert said in a soft, almost shameful voice.

"I see," Mrs. Happy replied. "No wonder you're complaining. He's in the lowest hundred."

"That's just what we're talking about," Sheriff Kramar said. "This Point System just seems to be causing trouble with the children, dividing them against—"

"What are the ranks of your children, Sheriff?" the old woman asked. The twinkle was now gone from her eye.

"That isn't the point here," Sheriff Kramar began.

"But of course it's the point," Mrs. Happy said. "I happen to know your children currently have no rank number at all. They won't even play the game. They haven't even been in my store since I put up the Big Board. I'm sure you're upset about such a thing, but I can't help it if they don't want to play. That's just the rules of the game. No play, no rank. Life just doesn't stop because a few people are poor sports and don't want to play."

"Who's making these rules, as you call them?" Sheriff Kramar asked in exasperation.

"Why the town, of course, and society in general," Mrs. Happy said. "That's always how the Point System works. No one complains that your children get graded on a test at school or that the school issues a report card. In fact, the only people that do seem to complain are the ones who don't do as well as the others, or the parents of those children who don't do well. My advice to you is to help your children do better. Your children are certainly talented enough, Sheriff. Surely you encourage them to play by the rules in life and perform as well as they can."

"Yes but—"

"Our whole society works this way, don't you see?" Mrs. Happy said. "It's performance that counts. As a lawman, you know the jails are full of those persons who break the law, who didn't perform up to accepted standards."

"In a way, you have a point," the sheriff nodded. "But this all seems so . . . so vague. I mean, who enters all the data into this Big Board? Scores and point totals seem to change on the hour. I've never seen anything like it."

"Well, people and situations change on the hour," Mrs. Happy said and laughed sympathetically. "But you have a good question. Unfortunately, it's all too technical and complicated for an old woman like me. My late husband understood computers, rest his soul. But as for me, well, I don't know much about it. I only know they work. But I can tell you that Goliath Industries has all the exclusive patents on the Big Boards."

"But how do they enter information?" Sheriff Kramar demanded. Then he sighed.

"Well, that would be telling trade secrets, and I can't do that," Mrs. Happy said and smiled sweetly. "But I can tell you they are very advanced scientifically. The Big Board just records things as they are. I mean, all the information is just common knowledge in this town. The Big Board is really doing this community a service by teaching the children at a young age what is expected of them. Now who can complain about a gift like that?"

"But my Nicolas is ranked in the bottom hundred!" Mrs. Hubert moaned. "That's just not fair! He's such a delicate child."

"So now we are getting honest, aren't we?" Mrs. Happy said with a grin. "You're ashamed that your little boy can't quite make the grade, aren't you?"

"That's not it at all," she said, tears coming to her eyes. "He's such a fragile child. Why must there be such a ranking to begin with?"

"That's not for me to decide," Mrs. Happy said simply. "As I said before, I don't make the rules. The Point System has always been in place. The Big Board is just a service to help 'clarify' where the children need improvement. Goliath Industries has found them very helpful. In fact, they use Big Boards in all their places of business. It's a great management tool."

"You mean more of these Big Boards are in operation?" Sheriff Kramar asked.

"Of course, they're everywhere," Mrs. Happy said. "I would think you'd know that. After all, Goliath is one of the biggest corporations in the world. This is just a small Big Board, actually. The one going up in the new factory will be much larger and much more comprehensive. I also might add that several police departments have found Big Boards quite useful too. I really would love to chat some more with you all, but I do have an appointment out at the factory."

The old woman ushered Sheriff Kramar and the others toward the door. A long black limousine was waiting at the curb in front of the store. A man in a gray uniform got out and opened the back door.

"We still haven't settled this problem, Mrs. Happy," Sheriff Kramar said as he walked out onto the sidewalk.

"I can see that, Sheriff," the old woman replied, looking straight into his eyes. "But you might want to remember that the children are playing along with the Point System with great dedication. Most parents appreciate the Point System too. They see the value. They want their children to improve themselves, to be the best they can be. But there's always a few poor-sport parents whose children don't quite make the grade."

"It's not a case of just being poor sports," Sheriff Kramar said. "I don't think the identity of our children should depend on—"

"I really must run, Sheriff," the old woman said. "But if I were you, I'd check around town before you begin attacking the Big Board and Goliath Industries. These are hard times and Goliath is helping this town. I don't need to remind you that elections are coming up in just a few months. What better example could you have of the Point System in action than our noble tradition of free elections? I'd be careful whom you criticize if I were you. If you rock the boat too much, you may just end up in the water."

"Is that some kind of threat, Mrs. Happy?" Sheriff Kramar asked. His face was red.

"Just an observation," the old woman said sweetly. "But surely I'm not telling you something you don't already know, am I? I must be running along. Good day." The old woman smiled once more, then got into a waiting limousine. The little group of parents stood silently on the sidewalk and watched the car drive away.

Daniel was upstairs in his room that Saturday evening. Night was falling. He was looking out his window at the street when he saw John and Susan Kramar pedal slowly by on their Spirit Flyer bicycles. They stopped at the end of the block and were talking to each other, looking at his house. John Kramar was shaking his head. Daniel wondered what they were saying. Then they rode back slowly toward his house. When they parked in front on the sidewalk, Daniel was up in a flash. He ran downstairs. His mother was in the kitchen, out of sight of the front door. Denise was in the living room.

The doorbell rang before Daniel could get there. Daniel flung the door open so quickly that Susan seemed startled.

"Hi," Daniel said, out of breath. "Before you say anything, I want you to know that things aren't like they seem, with the Cobra Club and everything. I mean, I'm trying to work things out, but it's complicated."

"Well, I wondered," Susan said carefully. She stared at Daniel, but he couldn't read her expression. "It seems like you've been avoiding us. But that's not unusual since the Point System started. We've got to talk. Something is up and we need your help. Tonight. You've got to get your Spirit Flyer and help us. We need more riders."

Just then, Denise stuck her head out the door. She looked at Susan and John, then walked back through the house.

"She'll tell my mother," Daniel fretted, watching Denise go into the kitchen. "What do you need help for?"

"Something is going to happen tonight, we think," Susan said in a whisper. "We only got glimpses of it from the mirrors on our bikes. But we're almost sure this is the night. And we can maybe stop it if we have more Spirit Flyers helping us. So you need to come with us tonight."

"I'd like to help," Daniel said honestly.

"Daniel!" Mrs. Bayley said. She pushed open the door. She stared at Susan quietly for a moment and then sighed. "So it is these children. I'll not have this sneaking around behind my back, young lady."

"No one is sneaking anything," Daniel said, his face crimson with embarrassment. Mrs. Bayley kept staring at Susan and her Spirit Flyer.

"I'll not have my son's head filled with this kind of nonsense," his mother said sharply. "Now take those ridiculous bicycles and leave the premises."

Susan nodded and turned around. John Kramar stared at Daniel's mother in surprise. "What's eating her?" he whispered.

"Let's just get out of here," Susan said softly.

Daniel stood in the doorway as Susan and John rode away. More than anything he wished he could follow them and help them.

"Really, Daniel. I'm disappointed in you," his mother said. "I thought you knew my feelings about those children."

Daniel didn't answer as he stared out after the two riders. His mother shut the door as she pulled him back inside.

Just outside of town, the black limousine that had carried Mrs. Happy was parked in front of the main building at the Goliath Industries factory. Though the factory was mostly dark, there was activity inside the boiler room.

A small isinglass window stuck in the heavy iron door showed the raging fire inside the largest boiler. Standing near the big furnace, two figures stood talking in the flickering orange light. One was Mrs. Happy and the other was Cyrus Cutright, the old executive manager of the factory.

"Sheriff Kramar and a few others came to complain about the Big Board," the old woman said.

"I saw the whole thing from my office," the thin man said and nodded. "The ones doing the worst always whine the loudest. It's the same old story. But that will change soon enough. They'll have bigger worries than the Point System after this Monday."

"The arrangements including this town bank have gained approval, then?" Mrs. Happy asked.

"Of course," Mr. Cutright said with a voice like a rusty door hinge. "Not only here but all over the whole country. This will be a feast. By the end of next week, Goliath and other ORDER businesses will have gained control over thousands of hurting banks, not to mention the businesses that fall in the aftermath."

"The fear factor should be ripe then," Mrs. Happy said.

"More than ripe, absolutely rotten," Mr. Cutright said with a smile. "When you threaten their money, the fear boils hot and sticky as tar. Centerville has qualified to receive four thousand more Z-14s to do the job."

"Only Z-level?" Mrs. Happy asked with a frown.

"I made the usual complaints, but this is a huge operation, not only here, but all over the world," Mr. Cutright said. "As I mentioned, this may be one of the biggest worldwide operations of all time. All units on all levels are assigned. None of us were prepared. But there should be enough fear to go around for all. They'll find it easy to attach. We'll all be eating ashes on this one."

A row of sealed red boxes were stacked neatly on pallets near the big boiler. Mr. Cutright lifted one of the boxes and set it at his feet. He cut the seal with his fingernail and opened the flaps. The box was filled to the top with writhing black snakes. One rose up in the air like a cobra. On the throat was a white X inside a white circle. The snake hissed, opening its mouth. The sharp fangs oozed a dark gooey substance that looked like liquid hate. Mr. Cutright pushed the snake down and closed the box.

"They're packing twenty Z-14s to a box these days," he said with a smile. The stack of boxes seemed to vibrate as muffled hisses were heard.

"And they recommend a fire release?" the old woman asked.

"We'll get better, more even distribution over the whole town in the smoke," Cyrus Cutright replied. "We just dump them in. They're also harder to detect by any possible snoopers too."

Mrs. Happy nodded as she stared at the shaking red boxes. The snakes inside knew it was time. They were eager to meet the fires of freedom. Mr. Cutright opened the door of the boiler. The flash of flames didn't seem to faze the thin man. He threw the whole box inside. A great hiss filled the air as the box burst into flames. Thick black smoke poured out along with streams of black tarry liquid. The liquid bubbled and boiled into more smoke. Mrs. Happy handed the old man another box which he heaved into the fire.

As the fire grew hotter, they threw in more boxes, faster and faster. They were both laughing by the time the last box burst into flames.

The black smoke poured out of the top of the tall factory smokestack. It had been over fifteen years since the big furnace had been used. No

one was meant to see the smoke. An occasional ember flew up in the air, glowing hot orange before dying. The moon was still down and the sky was churning with heavy clouds. A wind blew toward the east, carrying the smoke toward town.

But someone was watching. High in the sky, a girl and a boy on two old red bicycles saw the smoke coming. They had been sitting two hundred feet up in the sky, as if sitting in chairs. The bikes were motionless.

In the darkness, the smoke blew quickly. They smelled the awful odor first. "It smells like rotten eggs and burning tires," Susan Kramar said, covering her mouth.

"Turn on your light!" John Kramar yelled.

The Spirit Flyers were equipped with old headlights with a simple switch. For a moment the thick smoke seemed to be cut by the bright light. But then, as if powered by weak batteries, the lights grew dim. The cloud of smoke closed back in around the children.

"I can't breathe," John gasped.

"We've got to get out of here," Susan yelled and then coughed. She aimed the handlebars toward the ground and began to pedal. John followed her and the smoke blew faster right behind them. A rumble and a screeching noise came out of the cloud as they sped across the sky over the town. Susan looked back once and saw two enormous red eyes behind her. She pedaled faster in retreat, wondering why the lights didn't work like before.

By the time the children had landed in the driveway at their house, the smoke was falling all over the town like a stinky fog.

"I knew we needed help," John said. He pushed his Spirit Flyer into the garage. Susan was right behind him. She shut the door.

"Three of us might have made a difference," Susan said, her chest heaving. She slapped her clothes, trying to get rid of the dark presence she still felt was all over her like some kind of invisible slime. "That was awful. My light just went dim it seemed, like it ran out of power."

"The generators!" John blurted out. "Maybe that's how you use them. We've never really known how they work."

Susan cocked her head, thinking to herself. She reached over and touched the little bottle-shaped instrument that was attached to the framework of the rear tire.

"You may be right," she said. "Let's go try them."

She opened the big garage door quickly. The smoke was gone. Only a faint smell of rotten eggs and tar lingered in the dark night. Both children knew immediately that whatever had been done was done. They stared up at the dark cloudy sky, wondering what had come over their town so quickly.

THE DAY
THE FEAR
SPREAD
· · · · · · · ·

12

A fierce rain started on Saturday night after the smoke came out of the factory. The storm continued all day Sunday. But on Monday morning the sun was shining once more. Though it seemed like another normal day in Centerville, something deeper was happening to the town. In the months ahead, people would look back and remember that this was the day everything really began to change.

After breakfast, Daniel finished reading a book about space probes and the newest kinds of satellite weapons. He had read most of the book that weekend. His sister had already gone out that morning to a friend's house. Daniel sighed uncomfortably as he looked at the two bicycles in his garage. After staring at them a long time, he decided to walk to the library instead of riding either bicycle.

As he walked along the street, the sun was already starting to get hot. Yet there was something different in the air that the boy couldn't put his finger on. Things seemed unusually quiet. As he turned on Tenth Street and walked toward the town square, he got an eerie feeling that something was wrong.

For one thing, a man in a car backed out of his driveway so fast that Daniel had to jump out of the way. The car then screeched toward downtown going faster than the speed limit. Though Daniel had only been in Centerville just over a week, he knew most people didn't rush like they did in the city.

As he got closer to the square, an older woman was walking briskly toward him. As she passed Daniel, she didn't even look at him. Her face and eyes were red as if she'd been crying, and she was mumbling to herself. Daniel stopped and turned to watch her. Something inside told him that the woman was afraid.

Daniel began to slowly run along. As he got to the library, he was surprised to find a hastily scrawled note stuck to the front door. The note said, "Temporarily closed."

Daniel was thinking about the note when he heard a police siren. It seemed to be coming from the town square, so Daniel ran in that direction. When he got to the corner, he saw the commotion. A mass of people were crowded up in front of the Centerville Bank on the north side of the square. The siren stopped. Cars were parked helter-skelter in the street, blocking traffic. People were shouting and talking. More adults were running up from all directions. A man in a uniform was on the front steps of the bank trying to talk to the people.

"I wonder if there's been a robbery," Daniel said to himself. He ran toward the crowd, forgetting about his limp. As he got closer, he could feel the fear in the air, it was so thick. Something was wrong. He wondered if someone had been hurt. Daniel ran up to an older man in blue overalls who was standing in the back of his pickup truck so he could get a better look.

"What happened?" Daniel yelled up at the man. The man didn't seem to notice him. Daniel then ran into the crowd. Sheriff Kramar was yelling at people from the front steps of the bank.

"What happened?" Daniel asked a woman in a blue dress. "Has there been a robbery?" The woman looked down at Daniel impatiently as he pulled on her arm. "Has there been a robbery?" Daniel repeated.

"No, the bank is closed," the woman said. Then she looked up and yelled something.

"The bank is closed?" Daniel said to himself. He thought for a moment. "So what?"

He wormed his way through the crowd. He saw George the deputy in his wheelchair up on the steps by Sheriff Kramar. George held a shotgun across his lap. The deputy was watching the crowd carefully.

"I'm sure you'll be getting your money, Jessie," Sheriff Kramar was shouting at someone in the crowd. Daniel shoved his way through the bodies. Most of the adults didn't even seem to notice the boy, even when he stepped on their toes.

Daniel kept pushing and squeezing through holes until he got up to the front of the crowd. George looked at him but didn't smile. "You better go on home," George said quickly. "This is no place for a kid. The bank is closed and this could get ugly. Go on, now."

Daniel was about to ask a question, but saw that it was probably useless. He inched his way back through the crowd still rather confused by all the commotion. You could almost smell the fear, like a rotten thing. When he finally broke free, he saw more people, mostly adults, driving or running toward the bank from all directions.

Then he saw a black limousine move slowly down Tenth Street. For a moment, he thought he saw his mother in the back seat of the long black car, but as he ran closer, the car sped up and moved on.

Daniel stood on the south edge of the square for some time, just watching the people gather around the bank. Then he noticed Mrs.

Gardener, the head librarian, walking up the library steps. Daniel ran to catch up.

She was locking the door from the inside when Daniel knocked on the glass. "We're closed," she said.

"But I want to know what's going on," Daniel yelled so she could hear him through the glass. Mrs. Gardener hesitated and then opened the door. Daniel walked in and she locked the door. "Everyone says the bank is closed, but what's the big fuss about?" Daniel said.

Mrs. Gardener walked over to the library desk so slowly that she seemed half asleep. She picked up a newspaper and gave it to Daniel. He stared at the bold black headline: "BANK FAILURES FEARED! Money Panic Hits Major Cities!"

Mrs. Gardener slumped down into her chair and put her face down into her hands. Her shoulders shook for a moment. Daniel got more and more afraid as he watched. He started to read the story in the newspaper. Though he didn't understand all the talk about national debts and the banking systems and failures, he slowly began to realize why people were so afraid. Most people kept their money in the banks. When banks went out of business, they were afraid they would lose all their money. Mrs. Gardener looked up.

"I remember the Great Depression," she said softly. "I was only a little girl then, but I remember. They say this will be worse . . . much worse . . . so many rumors of wars . . ."

Daniel quickly read more of the newspaper as Mrs. Gardener seemed to stare out into space. All the stories seemed to be about money, inflation, banks and problems in the government. There were also a lot of news items about wars between countries with hard-to-pronounce names fighting each other over tariffs, shipping lanes, oil production and other things. Daniel was a good reader, yet he didn't quite understand what everything meant. All he knew was that things in the world and even in Centerville, had somehow gotten bad in a very short time.

"I better go home and see what my mother says about all of this stuff,"

Daniel said finally. Mrs. Gardener nodded. She walked wearily to the front door and unlocked it for him. Daniel had run halfway up the block when he realized he still had the book on space probes under his arm. He quickly decided to just keep running.

Daniel and Denise had already fixed sandwiches and soup for lunch by the time their mother arrived. Denise was quite scared when Daniel filled her in on all the things he had read. He had also been watching the news on television. All of the big stations and TV channels had interrupted the regular programs with news bulletins and stories. Daniel listened to the talking politicians and business leaders and tried to understand what was happening.

His mother walked into the house. She looked tired, the boy thought. She put down her briefcase and plopped down into a chair at the kitchen table.

"A lot of bad stuff is happening all over, isn't it?" Daniel asked his mother as he pushed a bowl of soup in front of her.

"Yes, there's trouble," she said carefully. "But it's not the end of the world."

"But I heard there's all these wars and things," Denise whined. "I'm scared, Mommy. Will it happen here too?"

Denise pushed her own chair closer to her mother's. Mrs. Bayley reached out and patted her arm.

"Not in Centerville," her mother said. "It's not that bad in our country. Only the banks and businesses are in trouble."

"Is our money in the Centerville Bank?" Daniel asked.

"Yes, it is," Mrs. Bayley said. "Or at least most of it is deposited there. However, Mr. Cutright down at the factory said there's nothing to worry about. He even said that Goliath Industries will probably buy the bank."

"So we won't lose our money?" Daniel asked.

"Of course not," Mrs. Bayley said. "He said it will reopen in a day or two, and then things will be back to normal, more or less. The government is helping out."

"All the stores are closed," Daniel said. "And even the big supermarket is closed, I heard."

"You're right," his mother said. "Apparently some problems were reported in another town and the store owners got scared that they might happen in Centerville."

"They showed some pictures on TV of all these people breaking the big glass windows of a supermarket with baseball bats and taking stuff right out of—"

"Let's not talk about that now," Mrs. Bayley said to Daniel. She nodded her head toward Denise who was staring at her bowl of soup. "In a few days this will all blow over and things will be back to normal."

"I don't see what a bunch of dumb problems those little countries are fighting about have to do with us," Denise said. "Who cares if they blow themselves up?"

"One problem is oil," Daniel said. "The Middle East countries are the main suppliers. Since those bombs went off and stopped the oil, the newsman on TV said it's causing a chain reaction of panic in other places. He said something about a debt bubble bursting that the government can't fix."

Mrs. Bayley nodded her head and looked anxious. She appeared lost in thoughts.

"There have been several oil crises. No one thought it could get this bad though," she said. "This one has triggered other things, they say, like the debt of the smaller nations and so on."

"But the bigger problem is the banks and money," Daniel said. "I was reading in the newspaper how the banking system is all connected. It said it was like a house of cards and when the bottom card falls, then all the other cards—"

"Let's not talk about it right now," Mrs. Bayley said. "All this talk of war just gives me the creeps. The people who know about these things will work it out. The government is taking measures. They'll make things better again. And large companies like Goliath Industries are helping too. In fact, Goliath is a leader in a whole group of major companies that is called ORDER. These businesses are taking a leading role in trying to keep things from getting out of hand. ORDER brings order, they are saying."

"I wonder if it will work," Daniel said. "I was reading that this century has had more wars and casualties than all the previous centuries combined. They also said we have enough bombs to blow the world up more than—"

"Let's not talk about it," Mrs. Bayley said. She stared at Daniel. "You'll scare Denise. And yourself. And me. Our money is safe, thanks to Goliath Industries. Taking that job with them was one of the best things I ever did, let me tell you."

"They're a really big company, aren't they?" Daniel said. "In fifteen years they've bought up hundreds of small companies so that they're one of the biggest companies in the world now. They mentioned Goliath Industries in the newspaper too."

"They're in the top ten in size," Mrs. Bayley said. "And that's security. So we shouldn't worry about the banks or bombs or any of that stuff, should we?"

"Not me," Denise said. But Daniel didn't answer.

"Why don't you go watch a little TV and just stay inside the rest of the day?" Mrs. Bayley said.

"Only scary stuff is on TV," Denise grunted. "And I can't even call my friends because the phones are messed up. Everything is busy or you don't get any sound."

"I know," Mrs. Bayley said. "People are just a little frightened right now. Things will be better tomorrow once the shock wears off. I've got to go back to the factory. We've got plenty of security with Goliath. In fact, we've been given the go-ahead to open earlier than planned so we can start production. We've got enough orders to last us two years already, Mr. Cutright said. He doesn't seem the least worried."

"The government needs the defense weapons and stuff Goliath is making, don't they?" Daniel asked. "No wonder your boss is happy."

"I didn't say he was happy, Daniel," Mrs. Bayley replied. "Don't be so critical. Like I said, if we are headed for hard times, Goliath is the place to be working. They're big enough to weather any storm. Centerville is lucky to have them in this town. Very lucky."

Denise left the table quietly. She had only taken two bites from her sandwich. Daniel heard her running up the stairs.

"Save that sandwich in the refrigerator," Mrs. Bayley instructed Daniel. "We may need it later. I'll go talk to Denise."

Even though Daniel felt puzzled and somewhat scared by all the recent changes on the news, he was still hungry. He ate his lunch, then put the rest of the leftover food in the refrigerator. His mother usually just threw leftover food down the garbage disposal.

Mrs. Bayley came downstairs fifteen minutes later. She gave Daniel a long silent hug. "You stay around the house," she said. "And just to be safe, keep the doors locked. Denise is taking a nap. I may be home a little late, but I'll try to get through on the phone if that happens."

"Ok," Daniel said. "I can watch TV or read."

"Just don't let Denise watch news that's too violent," Mrs. Bayley said. "And don't believe everything you hear."

Mrs. Bayley walked quickly out the front door. Daniel locked it. Then he checked the back door and locked it and then the garage doors. Locking all the doors made Daniel feel like he was on an important adventure almost. For a while he pretended he was a character in a book, like someone in the middle of a war zone, protecting his house from the enemy. Somehow it helped to make it all seem like a game.

He got a big glass of ice tea and a book. Then he turned on the television with the remote control. The newspeople looked serious and were still talking. Daniel looked down at his book on the wildlife of North America and sipped his tea. Occasionally he would glance up at the TV screen when something exciting was happening. They repeated the same pictures of the people breaking into a supermarket several times. They also showed the pictures of crowds of people in front of banks in different cities all over the world.

All the bad news on television and in the newspaper had always seemed so far away and distant. But the closed Centerville Bank and other stores had brought the news to his town. Daniel took another sip of ice tea. He wondered whether or not there would be soccer practice that night.

"I wonder if people lose points on the Big Board if they don't practice?" he asked himself. That's when he remembered the Point System and the warnings the Kramar children had spoken of on Saturday night. He switched off the TV so he could think. Under other circumstances, he would have gone back downtown to see if the toy store was open. But that would have to wait, he thought. He turned the TV back on. There was a picture of a building on fire, blazing out of control.

GETTING
A POINT
BREAKDOWN
· · · · · · · ·
13

By Wednesday, things had settled down somewhat in the little town of Centerville. The Centerville Bank re-opened that morning.

A town meeting had been called on Tuesday night down at the high-school gymnasium and the place had been packed, Daniel's mother had said. The news had been grim at first. The bank president had said that the government insurance programs had failed since a record number of banks were in trouble. There just wasn't enough money to cover nearly all the banks in the country. Then Mr. Cutright had announced that Goliath Industries had bought the local bank. Each depositor would lose a small percentage of his money. But even with the losses, the townspeople had cheered for fifteen minutes. Losing a little money was better than losing all of it. Mr. Cutright had then announced that there would be even more job positions opening at the factory than first anticipated. The crowd had cheered again. Many people had lost their jobs in the past two days.

Though Happy Toy Store had been closed on Monday and Tuesday, the doors were open on Wednesday morning. The other stores in town had opened too. The big supermarket had been packed. Daniel went early in the morning with his mother. People zoomed down the aisles, throwing food into their shopping carts in a frenzy. Like most everyone else in town, they bought three times the normal amount of groceries, especially canned goods. Some people complained that Mrs. Fairfax, the manager of the store, had raised the prices on nearly every item in the store. She also demanded cash. No checks or credit cards were accepted. A lot of people were complaining at her office, Daniel noticed. But Mrs. Fairfax, a large red-faced woman, told them if they didn't like it they could buy their food elsewhere. Most people went away grumbling, but they still bought their food first.

Everybody acted a little different, Daniel noticed. Even though things seemed to be more or less back to normal on the surface, Daniel could see the fear or a solemn seriousness on their faces. People seemed edgy and tense. His mother commented on it at the market. Nobody joked or smiled much. Everything was business, serious business.

"When will all this stuff get better?" Daniel asked his mother as they unpacked the groceries that morning.

"Well, right now no one seems to know for sure," Mrs. Bayley replied. Her face looked tired. "Nothing like this has ever happened in our country before. We've had at least one big depression before, but they say this is a much more complicated situation. Everyone thought the government was more prepared. And it doesn't help that so many little countries are at war. I don't know when it will get better. But at least I have a good job."

"I just hope you don't lose it," Daniel said.

"Don't worry. They like me at Goliath," Mrs. Bayley said. "I don't intend to mess up a good situation."

Daniel wondered what would happen if his mother lost her job. The more he thought about it, the less he wanted to know the answer.

Soccer practice resumed Wednesday evening. Daniel was curious to see the other guys on the team. They seemed just as serious as their parents. They either talked about the changes that had taken place in town or in the world. But more importantly they talked about the sudden changes in the Point System.

"Mike Weaver's dad lost his job yesterday and Mike dropped down two hundred and thirty-four rank places," Barry Smedlowe said. Mike was one of the boys on the Rockets' team. "Mike wasn't sure how many points he lost in the deal, but the whole thing looks real bad for him."

"The Big Board is still operating?" Daniel asked as he walked up to the other boys.

"Are you kidding?" Barry asked. "The toy store has been packed. Today was the first time you could get a complete Point Breakdown sheet. They're great. With a Point Breakdown you can see where each point fits into what they call your Personal Point Profile. Everything is right there in black and white, your strong areas and weak ones."

"But Point Breakdowns cost a dollar," Alvin complained. "My mom has cut off my allowance. She says we have to tighten our belts. She thinks we're all headed for real hard times with all the problems in the government."

"I just wish the Combo-Gizmos would do Point Breakdown printout sheets," Barry said sadly. "I could make a fortune. Two-thirds of the kids at the toy store were buying Point Breakdowns. I don't blame them either. Big changes have been happening on the Big Board since the bank closed and reopened. Luckily, I'm still solid as Number One. And the rest of the guys in the club are solid too. But the way things are changing, I don't know how long that will last."

"My dad was talking about moving to another town," Doug Barns said. He looked worried. "He may lose his job in Kirksville. The company he works for is in trouble. He went out to the new Goliath factory to check on jobs this afternoon. He said we're lucky they came to town."

"That's the truth," Barry replied. "My dad says big industry and government jobs are the most secure, and he should know since he's school principal. He says a lot of changes are coming. That's why it's important to be up in rank in the Point System."

"What about your Super Summer Party?" Alvin asked. "Are you still planning on having it?"

"Of course," Barry replied. "And that's going to be the only party in town that night. I've even got a plan that's going to make it a sure thing."

"What about the party at the town pool?" Daniel asked.

"There won't be one," Barry said and smiled.

Just then, Coach Goober came over. He was dressed in his gym shorts and was carrying a clipboard.

"Listen up!" he yelled and then blew his whistle. "The people running the Goliath Sports League want you to know that even though there's been a few upsets around town the last few days and all, the League is still on schedule." The boys all cheered. The coach blew his whistle to get their attention. Daniel waited patiently. "Now, I know things look bad on TV in the world situation and all," Coach Goober began. He frowned so he looked like he had one big eyebrow. "But this is still a great country with a lot of fighting spirit, even in tough times. Like I said the first day, it's survival of the fittest. I want to see you guys playing like it's survival of the fittest. A lot of kids are trying to make Superstars. But there will only be two Superstar teams—one boys' and one girls'. Will you be on one of those teams?"

"Yes!" the boys screamed back.

"Then let's get out there and see some ball control, more offense and better defense. Do you hear me?"

"Yes!" they yelled again. This time even Daniel yelled just as loud as the rest of the guys.

After a grueling practice, Barry called a meeting of the Cobra Club over at his house. Daniel's mother was right there and accepted the invitation for Daniel. But he would have gone anyway, he decided, as he rode his Super Wings bicycle over to the big house. He felt only a twinge of betrayal as he rode the new ten-speed. He thought of going home to get the Spirit Flyer, but he knew that would just make his mother unhappy. Besides, he also knew the other boys would make fun of the old red bicycle.

In spite of his limp, Daniel had done well in practice that day. And since the other boys had learned the fundamentals of soccer a little better, the practices weren't quite as painful as the first week. A few of the boys even complimented Daniel when he made some good passes and traps. Even the coach seemed impressed.

The boys rode their bicycles together like a gang. Daniel felt good for a change and even accepted. The boys seemed more friendly than usual. They kidded him about being Rank Blank, but they weren't as cruel in their teasing. They parked their bikes in Smedlowe's garage.

"Daniel won't be Rank Blank for long," Barry said and winked.

"How do you know?" Daniel asked. He was suddenly more interested than he wanted to admit.

"Well, I don't know all the details yet, but Mrs. Happy said that the time was ripe for a change," Barry said. "She said that you can get on the Big Board and get a real rank any day now. All you have to do is go see her and find out how it's done."

"I wonder," Daniel said. He hadn't been in the toy store since the day the Big Board arrived.

"Inviting you to be a member in the Cobra Club has been a big help for all of us," Barry said. "Mrs. Happy told me that we all get credit on our scores for helping you out. And I saw it right there on the Point Breakdown sheet. It was under the 'Friend: Plus & Minus' category. You were a credit on the plus side."

"Really?" Daniel asked. He had wondered why the guys in the Cobra Club had been so nice to him that day. Suddenly it made more sense. They knew they were getting points on the Big Board for being nice. But somehow that didn't make Daniel feel as accepted as before. He wished he could get a close look at a Point Breakdown sheet.

"I noticed an odd thing too," Barry said. The president of the Cobra Club frowned. "The Point Breakdown sheet mentioned that you were on Level Two. Mrs. Happy said that since you owned a Goliath Super Wings bike that you qualified for Level Two. I'm not quite sure what all she meant, but I think that's supposed to be good. She said that you were the only Level Two person in town."

"If that's so great, then how come he's Rank Blank?" Alvin demanded and looked at Daniel suspiciously.

"She said that Daniel could get a rank number easy if he'd play by the rules of the Point System," Barry replied. "She said that you knew what the problem was. I wanted to see your Point Breakdown, but she wouldn't let me." Barry looked at Daniel. All the other boys were staring at him too. Daniel smiled nervously and looked down. "Anyway, she wants you to stop by and see her," Barry said. "She said it's real important to your future standing in this town."

The boys then began talking about the Superstar team and their chances for winning. Daniel was only half listening. The news that he might be able to get rid of his Rank Blank position had touched a desire deep inside the boy. As much as he hated the thought, he knew he would have to go back to the toy store and face the Big Board again. If the Point System was the only game in town, he wondered if it was time for him to play.

That evening, Denise came home with a Point Breakdown sheet. Daniel wanted to look at it, but Denise wouldn't let him. Instead, she took it straight to her mother. Mrs. Bayley had known in advance about Point Breakdowns and had decided she would pay for a printout once a week for both children.

"The company will pay for the Point Breakdowns for each worker at the factory," she said as she put a casserole on the kitchen table. "But our Big Board isn't installed yet."

"I wish I could get a Point Breakdown more often than just once a week," Denise said. She frowned down at the paper. She had been studying the columns of words and numbers and point totals for over an hour. Daniel sat down at the table and peeked at her sheet. He was surprised at what he read.

He didn't blame Denise for being secretive. The Big Board was very efficient in breaking down a person into categories and then breaking down the categories into specific items.

For example, the first category on the Point Breakdown was the all important: APPEARANCE. Getting a good score in Appearance was absolutely essential if you wanted to be in the top ranks in the Point System. The Point Breakdown sheet divided a person's appearance into several separate items. *Face* was the first item listed under Appearance. And under Face listing were other items, like smile rating, teeth, lips, chin, eyes, eye color, ears, skin complexion, makeup, wrinkles, dimples, nose, hair, hair color, hair length, hair style, and on it went.

But Face was only one category under Appearance. There were also the categories of Height and Weight and Proportion, almost like a doctor's chart. Many children were quite concerned about the Fatness Factor under the Weight category. A bad score in that department could be devastating on your overall rank in the Big Board.

Clothing was another listing under Appearance. That not only included shoes, pants and shirts, but also things like Style. Denise, like many boys and girls, was especially concerned about the Style listing and the Status Points for Name Brand Items. Many children had compared their Point Breakdown listings that day, and they soon discovered which clothes and shoes earned the most points on the Big Board. Everyone wanted their parents to buy those exact items. Denise was trying to show her mother the necessity of getting a new pair of shoes.

"All the kids are wearing the new Ten Toes shoes, Mom," Denise said to her mother.

"Those shoes cost twice as much as the ones you have now," Mrs. Bayley said. "And your shoes still have a lot of wear left in them. I just don't think we have the money these days. There are enough problems going on in the world without us having to buy you new shoes when we just bought shoes three weeks ago."

"That's not the point, Mom," Denise said. "Ten Toes shoes are the best thing. They cost a lot, but they're worth it. Carla Roberts got a new pair this afternoon and got all kinds of points for it. She improved two whole ranks in less than a half-hour. She showed me her Point Breakdowns before the shoes and after. I don't even think she looks all that cute in them. But I would look great. I tried some on. The woman who sold shoes said she thought I could improve at least three and maybe even four ranks if I had a new pair."

"Well, maybe," Mrs. Bayley said. "But we'll have to wait until the end of the month when I get my paycheck."

"Couldn't we get them sooner?" Denise whined. "I really want some. I'll just die if the other kids on my team all get them, and I'm the only one left out. I could even get knocked out of the Top One Hundred. You wouldn't want that to happen, would you?"

"Well, I'll think about it," Mrs. Bayley said. "But I'm not making any promises. I still think your other shoes are perfectly good, sensible shoes."

"They've gotten stained, and I can't clean them," Denise said. "And it's one of the lower ratings on my Point Breakdown, see?"

Denise shoved the print-out sheet under her mother's nose. Mrs. Bayley looked at the chart carefully. She nodded as she read the various items. "You scored a lot of points under Hair Style," Mrs. Bayley mused. "I knew that new cut was going to look better on you."

"Yeah, but look at the shoes part," Denise said. "See? I'm going downhill by the day with those old shoes of mine."

"Well, I told you I would think about it," Mrs. Bayley said. Then she looked at Daniel. "How are you doing?"

"You mean in general or on the Point System?" Daniel asked.

"Is there a difference?" his mother replied. She had a tired, almost disgusted look in her eyes. Her look made Daniel feel awful inside.

"Well, I'm trying," Daniel said, feeling defensive. "In fact, I'm supposed to go by and see Mrs. Happy tomorrow. Barry said that she said I could stop being Rank Blank, maybe."

"Anything would be an improvement," Mrs. Bayley said and sighed. "I just don't understand why it's taking you so long to fit in. Maybe I should go down there with you."

"No!" Daniel blurted out. "I mean, that would look horrible. Besides if you complain, I could be Rank Blank forever. It's not a good idea to complain."

"I realize that," his mother said. "That's why I haven't pressed the issue. But I still don't understand why a bright boy like you isn't getting credit on the Big Board. It's just not right."

"Maybe that will change," Daniel said hopefully. Looking at his mother's disappointed face cut deep into the boy. At that moment, he wished he was just a normal boy like all the others. He would have given anything to get into the Point System. He was tired of being on the outside all the time. He felt like he was a disappointment to his mother and a disgrace to his family. As much as he tried to shake off the poisonous bad feeling, it still hung on him as he limped off to bed.

A PAIN
IN THE
NECK
· · · · · · · · ·
14

Daniel woke up on Thursday morning feeling more confused than ever. All through the night, he had dreams of getting a rank on the Big Board. But in the dreams, he not only saw his name in lights up on the Big Board, he also saw himself trapped inside the Big Board. The boy had woken up in a sweat twice. He figured it was all just a dream. He still planned to go see Mrs. Happy as he got ready for breakfast.

Daniel limped downstairs slowly. His mother and sister were already at the kitchen table. "We should be getting a Big Board at the factory today," Mrs. Bayley said after finishing her cup of coffee.

"Do people at the factory have number cards too?" Denise asked.

"Mr. Cutright said they'll be processed right away," her mother replied. "Mr. Favor, the new manager, has used the Point System before and says it's a great management tool. He says it keeps people on their toes and working hard. That's good for everyone in these times."

"I wonder what's going to happen since everything is such a mess in the government," Denise said. "Everyone I know has been acting different since the bank closed and people got scared. People aren't as friendly."

"They're just worried," her mother explained. "It's natural to feel more stress in times like these. But don't you children worry. We'll ride this out."

Her mother left the table. Daniel ate slowly and finished by himself. Mrs. Jenkins came just as his mom left for the factory. She brought a shopping bag with her knitting in it.

The mail carrier left the mail a half-hour later. Daniel went outside to get it. Most of the mail was for his mother. Denise rushed over and grabbed a fashion magazine called *Pretty You* out of Daniel's hands. She had a two-year subscription and was a loyal reader of the make-up tips, fashion news and beauty comments.

"How come you read that stupid magazine?" Daniel asked. "You're only ten years old."

" 'You're never too young to look pretty,' " Denise said, quoting the magazine's motto. "And that's the truth. Did you know that Wanda Bishop got a big red pimple on the end of her nose this week and went down four ranks? We all saw her score in black and white on the Point Breakdown print-out sheet. There were big red negative points under the areas of Face, for nose and skin blemishes."

"All because of a pimple?" Daniel asked.

"Well it looked all red and awful and sort of oozed," Denise replied. "If she had used make-up, she could have kept her points, if you ask me. But that one pimple dropped her down to one hundred two in rank.

That means she's lost her invitation to the Top One Hundred party that Cindy and Craig are giving. That's just what one pimple can do. I hate to think what would happen if her whole face broke out."

Daniel shook his head, amazed that so much trouble could be caused by a single pimple. The boy rubbed his chin feeling for any bumps. Feeling safer when he didn't find any, he sorted through the rest of the mail. On the bottom of the pile was a letter addressed to him. There was no name or return address on the outside of the letter. The postmark was from the Centerville post office.

"Who wrote you?" Denise asked curiously.

"I don't know," Daniel said. He was about to open the letter when he thought maybe he should read it in private. He left the mail on the table and limped upstairs.

He closed the door of his room and ripped open the letter. He was surprised to see that the letter was from Susan Kramar. He began reading it slowly.

Dear Daniel,

I know your mother doesn't want you to see us, and it's probably because we have Spirit Flyer bicycles. I don't want you to get in trouble, so I'm writing this letter to fill you in on recent developments.

As you know, lots of stuff is happening in Centerville and it doesn't look good. The Big Board and Point System are just the beginning of something worse to come, we think. To make a long story short, John and I were warned by two different sources to beware of a coming deeper attack on Centerville.

The evening we came to your house we were trying to warn you and get you to help us fight back. We needed more power. That night the attack came in a great cloud of smoke that came from the Goliath factory. Something was in the smoke, something awful. It's hard to explain, and I don't know if you'd believe me even if I tried. You needed to see it. But believe me, people are acting more afraid and weird not only because the Point System is working but for other reasons too. The shadow over Centerville just gets worse and worse.

I guess your mother won't let you ride your Spirit Flyer. But I know you said you had Spirit Flyer Vision goggles. If you can, go out in the town and put them on. Look at people while wearing the goggles. The goggles may show you some of the deeper stuff we've been seeing and then you'll understand. Please, if at all possible, do this as soon as you get this letter.

We will be leaving today to visit our Grandfather Kramar. He may know more how to fight the Point System and all the things that have been happening in a deeper way.

Your friend in the Kingdom,

Susan Kramar

Daniel read the letter three times. Then he opened his closet door and got out an old locked, wooden box. He opened the lock and lifted the lid.

The Spirit Flyer Vision goggles were lying near the top. He dropped the letter in the box and locked it. He stuffed the goggles under his shirt and went downstairs. Denise was showing Mrs. Jenkins some of the face creams and make-up she wanted in the advertisements of *Pretty You* magazine.

"I'm going out for a while," Daniel said.

"Be back for lunch," Mrs. Jenkins said.

Daniel went in the garage. He looked at both bicycles. He wanted to ride the Spirit Flyer, but when he made a move for it, he felt a sudden stab of pain in his neck. He rubbed his neck slowly and decided he didn't need the old bike or the new one; he would just take the goggles.

He walked quickly, not even thinking about his limp. He headed downtown on Tenth Street as he usually did. As he got to the town square, he crossed the street to the middle of the square. The old bandstand was empty, so Daniel quickly walked up the steps. He stood near one of the wooden pillars that held up the gazebo-style roof.

He took a deep breath and carefully took the goggles from underneath his shirt. He looked around to see if anyone was watching. He quickly slipped the goggles on.

At first he could see nothing but darkness, as if the glass wasn't clear at all, like a dark welder's mask.

"Please work. I need you," Daniel said softly to himself. He had hardly ever used the goggles and each time he had, they had worked differently. He knew that you couldn't make them work. All you could do was put them on and ask the Kings to release their power in them so you could see.

Then the town suddenly came into focus out of the darkness. Daniel paid attention. The first thing he noticed was a shadowy darkness. It seemed especially dark over the bank, almost like a storm cloud. A man came out of the bank across the square and began walking toward the bandstand. As he got closer, Daniel saw a great dark thing on the man. The boy blinked and looked again. The man was still walking closer. This time Daniel saw the dark thing more clearly, but he found it hard to believe what he saw.

Daniel lifted up the goggles and rubbed his eyes. He looked at the man with normal eyes and then slipped the goggles back on. Then he lifted them up again, comparing what he saw. Without the goggles, the man just seemed to be normal. He looked worried and preoccupied, but that wasn't unusual around town anymore. But seeing deeper through the Spirit Flyer goggles, he saw a different sight. A great dark thing was wrapped around the man's neck and down his chest. As the man got closer, Daniel saw the darkness more clearly.

"The chain," Daniel whispered to himself. Then he looked deeper at the man. There was something else attached. The man walked right in front of Daniel. From behind, the boy could see more clearly. A sort of vibrating red spot was on the back of the man's head, like a sore about the diameter of a softball. Right in the middle of it was the head of a black snake. The snake's mouth was clamped down into the flesh like a leech. The body of the snake was tightly wrapped in and around the chain. Only the tail wiggled slightly at each step.

Daniel gasped and ripped off the glasses. The man looked normal again. Daniel was wondering about what he had seen when a woman crossed the street and walked toward the bandstand. Daniel slipped the goggles back on. The darkness on the woman was even heavier. As she passed by Daniel saw why. Three of the leechlike snakes were attached to a red place in the back of her neck and head. Each snake was a slightly different size. One was as thick as a pencil, about a foot long. Another one was about the size of a garden hose and three feet long. And the third one was much bigger, about as big around as Daniel's arm. It wrapped around the woman's neck and into the chain and was squeezed around her body like a boa constrictor. As the woman passed in front of Daniel, the biggest snake stopped biting. Daniel felt uneasy. The big snake turned and spread it's hood like a cobra as it stared straight at Daniel. A white X was inside a white circle on the snake's throat. The snake hissed at Daniel.

Just then, the woman stopped walking. She paused, then turned to look at Daniel. "What are you doing to that bandstand?" the woman asked angrily.

"Nothing," Daniel said with surprise. He pulled the goggles off quickly.

"I think I saw you cutting it with a pocketknife," the woman replied. "There's a law against vandalizing public property. Did you know that?"

"I wasn't doing anything," Daniel replied, his face turning red. The woman's bizarre behavior had caught him completely off guard.

"You're one of those new boys in town, aren't you?" the woman asked. "You better learn how we do things in Centerville, or we'll fix you."

With that, the woman turned and walked on down the sidewalk. Daniel was too overwhelmed to do anything but watch her leave. With some hesitation, he put the goggles back on. The big snake kept staring at Daniel as the woman walked away. But as she crossed the street to the other side of the town square, it seemed to have latched back onto the raw red splotch with the other snakes.

Daniel heard a noise and saw a group of younger children riding their bicycles on the sidewalk across the center of the square. He watched them carefully. He saw the heavy loose chains around their necks. As they passed by him, he saw more of the black snakes attached to the ugly red patches at the backs of their heads. All the children had at least one of the snakes hanging on like a parasite, and some had two.

Daniel took off the goggles and looked at the children. They appeared to be as normal as any other person. As Daniel looked down Main Street, he saw the Happy Toys sign blinking on and off in purple neon. He remembered he had planned to meet with the old woman.

Daniel walked quickly down the steps of the bandstand, stuffing the goggles under his shirt. Using the goggles had shown him something, but he wasn't sure what it all meant. He wished he could talk to Susan. She seemed to know more about the things of the Spirit Flyer.

Just then, the purple neon sign of Happy Toys caught the boy's eye. He stared at the blinking sign. For a moment, he was about to put the goggles back on to look at the store. But he felt a sudden pain in the back of his neck. While he rubbed his neck, he remembered that he had intended to go see Mrs. Happy.

"It won't hurt to see what she has to say," Daniel said to himself. He began walking toward the toy store almost mindlessly. As he walked, he tried to think about what he had just seen in the goggles. Yet as he tried to concentrate, he got a nagging ache in the back of his neck. He felt more confused as he walked.

He stopped in front of the big glass windows of the toy store, right below the buzzing, blinking sign. A great wave of fear came over the boy for a moment. For an instant, he just wanted to run away as fast as he could go. But as he turned to go, he felt another jolt of pain in his neck. He stopped to pause and rub his neck again. That's when he looked through the store windows and saw the Big Board. Daniel forgot his fear and the pains in his body as he stared at the mysterious dark panel.

"Maybe I'll just look at it with the goggles," he said to himself. He quickly opened the door and stepped into the cool, air-conditioned toy store. Daniel walked quietly toward the Big Board.

He stopped when he got in front of it. He touched the goggles underneath his shirt. At that moment he realized that deep inside, he wasn't sure he intended to use the goggles at all. What he really wanted was to see whether or not he had finally earned a rank. Once again, the fears of facing an unknown judgment gripped the boy. He wanted to run. But as he turned, he bumped right into Mrs. Happy. Daniel almost screamed. It seemed like she had just appeared out of thin air.

"Excuse me," he gasped. His whole body was shaking. A severe pain shot through his neck.

"I've been expecting you," the old woman said with a smile. "The Big Board has been waiting too."

Daniel nodded, trying to catch his breath. The old woman chuckled as she gently patted the top of his head.

FLIGHT
TO THE
FUTURE
• • • • • • • •
15

The toy store seemed empty. Daniel looked around. Not a child or grown-up was to be seen.

"You are a lucky boy," the old woman said with a twinkle in her eye. She turned and walked slowly to the front door. Daniel's eyes went wide when she turned the knob on the lock. He heard a click.

"Why are you locking up?" Daniel asked. He gulped down another wave of fear.

"I don't want us to be disturbed," Mrs. Happy said with a smile. "As I said, you are a lucky boy. I have something very special to show you."

"Oh?"

"Wait here," the old woman commanded. She walked to the back of the store and disappeared into her office. When she came back out, she was pushing a bicycle. At first Daniel didn't recognize that it was a Goliath Super Wings because of all the attachments. Several odd-looking gadgets were on the handlebars. The only one that Daniel had seen before was a Combo-Gizmo.

"I have here a fully loaded, top-of-the-line Goliath Super Wings with all the extras," Mrs. Happy said. She knocked down the kickstand. "Take a look. Better yet, get on the seat and see how it feels. This is the bike of the future. The question is whether or not you'll be a part of the future. I need to get one more item."

The old woman walked back to her office. Daniel stared at the brand new bike and then moved closer to inspect it. The gadgets on the handlebars pricked his interest the most. The oddest-looking attachment was a rather plain black box about seven inches square. It was mounted right in the center of the handlebars. A white circled X was on the side facing the rider. Daniel bent over for a closer look.

"Go ahead and get on the bike," Mrs. Happy instructed. Daniel jumped. He hadn't heard the old woman walk over. He turned to say something but instead stared at what she was holding. A small bird cage was in her hand. And inside the cage was a very nervous brown-and-black sparrow.

"Is that a pet?" Daniel asked.

"No. It's a wild bird," the old woman said. "They have to be wild to work."

"Work for what?" Daniel asked.

"Fuel, of course," Mrs. Happy said. She stared hard into his eyes. "Get on the bike and I'll show you something you've never ever seen before."

Daniel stared back into the strange eyes of the old woman. He swung a leg over and sat on the seat of the Super Wings bike. As soon as he sat down, the Big Board suddenly came alive. Numbers and words flashed by at a dizzying speed. Then it stopped in a an electric hum, the lights frozen into words:

****

WELCOME TO THE BIG PICTURE TOUR, DANIEL BAYLEY!!!

****

While Daniel was trying to understand what the words meant, Mrs. Happy was reaching into the bird cage. The little sparrow squawked and sputtered as it tried to escape her hand. She trapped it in a corner of the cage.

"Hold on tight," the old woman commanded as she stepped over toward the bike. The bird was gripped tightly in the old woman's fingers. Daniel reached automatically for the handlebars. The bird's little black eyes were shiny with fear as she pushed it toward the odd black box on the handlebars.

Daniel heard a voice call his name. He looked up and saw himself in the Big Board. The reflection was on a bicycle and had a long chain wrapped around his neck. On the chain he could see a heavy dark lock. Though the lock on the chain was broken open, the boy seemed to feel the weight of the chain growing heavier and heavier by the second. Then suddenly he noticed that the chain in the reflection came right out of the Big Board toward him. The little bird chirped once. Daniel looked down. At that instant, Mrs. Happy pushed the bird toward the white circled X. The circle seemed to open by itself as the bird was soundlessly sucked inside the box. Then the circle closed.

A wild look was in the old woman's eyes. "The blood of one wild bird will give you enough time for the tour," she said.

Before Daniel could say a word, the Goliath Super Wings rose up off the floor of the toy store. Daniel gripped the handlebars in surprise and fear. The boy's reflected image pulled on the chain. Both boy and bicycle shot straight toward the Big Board as the reflected image pulled Daniel in. Daniel yelled, bracing himself for a crash, but the crash never came.

He heard a popping sound, like a cork being pulled from a bottle. Then he was through, zipping through the darkness. At first he couldn't see anything, but he could feel wisps of things all around him. Then the darkness began to fade. Daniel found himself riding down a street in a town. Then he recognized that the town was Centerville, but it seemed different somehow, as if it weren't quite all solid. Objects seemed vaporish or ghostlike. The buildings and parked cars seemed watery thin, almost two dimensional. The colors weren't as bright as they should have been. A few people were walking on the sidewalks, and they too seemed flat and thin, like wet cartoons.

The Super Wings bicycle flew three-feet high in the air, right down the middle of Main Street. That's when Daniel saw the toy store. The door opened and he saw Mrs. Happy rolling another Super Wings bicycle outside. Her Super Wings was loaded with attachments just like the one Daniel was riding. She had a bird in her hand. She pushed the bird toward the black box. The bird was instantly sucked in. Mrs. Happy got on the bike and pedaled up into the air toward Daniel.

"Happy to see me?" she asked with a laugh. "Welcome to the future of your dreams."

"Why is Centerville so different?" Daniel asked.

"Because it isn't your time yet," the old woman replied. "Follow me." The old woman reached over and grabbed the chain that hung on Daniel. She aimed her bicycle higher and flew up over the row of buildings on Main Street, dragging Daniel captive behind her. Even up high, everything seemed dreamishly thin.

"The Superstar awards ceremony has started," the old woman said. "And you're Number One at last."

"What?" Daniel asked.

High in the air, Daniel could see the rows of parked cars and trucks in the school parking lot. A shout and a cheer went up in the distance. The riders sailed silently closer. Soon the boy and woman were over the athletic field. A great crowd was in the bleachers. In front of them were long tables full of food and drinks. And beyond the tables was a long platform. A row of boys were lined up on one side and a row of girls on the other. And behind all that was the Big Board mounted on two large poles. Lights were flashing on and off in big purple letters.

****

DANIEL BAYLEY: THE NUMBER ONE SUPERSTAR!!!

****

The crowd went wild in a cheer when a boy with red hair walked across the platform. He stood next to a man who was holding a microphone. Daniel's mouth dropped open when he realized the boy was himself.

"That's me!" Daniel said.

"And all those cheers are for you," the old woman said with a smile. "That's because you're Number One and a Superstar. You have the highest rank among all the children in town."

"Really?" Daniel asked. "How did I get a rank?"

"You finally smartened up," Mrs. Happy said. "You saw a vision of what the future could be like and you accepted the inevitable."

"I did?" Daniel asked. He couldn't believe his eyes. The people in the crowd leaped to their feet with a standing ovation. And in the crowd in the front row, Daniel saw his mother. A huge beaming smile was on her face as she clapped for her boy. She was radiant with happiness.

"Just let that applause soak in," Mrs. Happy said and smiled. She braked her bicycle in midair, right over the platform. Daniel looked down at himself. Even though he was thin and watery, the stuff of dreams, the applause sure sounded real from where he was sitting in the sky. The Daniel on the platform was holding a trophy. He looked up and seemed to see Mrs. Happy and the real Daniel up in the air. The thin, ghostlike Daniel smiled broadly and held up the trophy as the crowd cheered. The Big Board was flashing a message of congratulations.

Mrs. Happy smiled as she watched Daniel. Then she looked at the black box attached to the handlebars of his bike. The white circled X on the box began to glow on and off.

"Time to go," Mrs. Happy said. "Your fuel is running out."

Daniel didn't want to leave that place or moment in time. The sound of the applause was the music of acceptance and approval. He hadn't heard such a sweet sound since the time he had been nine and made the All-City soccer team. This sounded even better. He felt as if he could have listened to it forever. Then the bike began to fall.

Mrs. Happy aimed her bicycle for the Big Board. Daniel did the same. As he shot down lower, he noticed the white circled X glowing on and off. The boy braced himself as the bike flew toward the headlines on the Big Board proclaiming him the Number One Superstar. Daniel blinked as the bike sailed right into the darkness of the mysterious panel.

As the darkness lifted, he could see shelves of toys in the distance, as if they were at the end of a long tunnel. Before he could think about it, the bike carried him through the other side of the Big Board with a slight popping sound. The bike crashed to the floor of the toy store and Daniel went sprawling. A shot of pain went through Daniel's right leg as the pedal on the bicycle tore into his pants. The bike was sideways on the floor, the front wheel silently spinning.

Mrs. Happy walked over. She held out her hand to help him up. Daniel grasped her cold hand and struggled to his feet. Mrs. Happy picked up the Super Wings bicycle and parked it on the kickstand.

"That was a short tour of your future, my boy. And as you see, you play a big part in the Big Picture of Centerville." The old woman walked around the bike. She bent over the handlebars. She held her left hand underneath the square black box while she pushed the center of the circled X. A short hiss and a puff of smoke came from the box as a gray powder dropped into the woman's left hand. The powder looked like ashes to Daniel. She scooped them quickly into her mouth.

"What was that?" Daniel asked.

"Just cleaning out the Trag 7 power unit," Mrs. Happy replied. She wiped her mouth with the back of her hand. Daniel stared at her.

"What happened to the bird?" Daniel asked.

"We haven't got time for birds," the old woman said quickly. "Let's be honest. How did you like the tour and the sound of all that applause? It was music to your ears, wasn't it?"

"It was rather nice."

"Nice? You loved it," Mrs. Happy said. "Deep down, I showed you what you want for your future, didn't I, my boy? The Goliath Super Wings took you right to the place of your dreams and desires."

"I guess so," Daniel said slowly.

"And what a bright future it is, my boy, *if and only if* you play by the rules of the game." The old woman stared at him right in the eyes.

"How could I ever be Number One, though?" Daniel asked. "Barry's Number One."

"But you have a Goliath Super Wings bicycle," Mrs. Happy said. "As you can see, they are very special bicycles when properly equipped. Owning a Super Wings qualifies you for Level Two in the Point System. That's the rules. And anyone on Level Two is automatically ahead of those people on Level One. If you would look at your Point Breakdown under the category of Possessions, you would see the value of the Super Wings. It's the bike of the future, my boy. And it's the bike in your future, isn't it?"

"But what about my Spirit Flyer?" Daniel asked, suddenly remembering the old red bicycle.

"That old bike?" Mrs. Happy snorted. "Why there's no comparison between that junk heap and a fully loaded, totally equipped, modern Super Wings. Wise up, child. That old bike is just an embarrassment that's holding you back from reaching your true potential."

"But it's a gift from the Three Kings," Daniel said.

"Nonsense and lies," the old woman replied. "Get in on the wave of the future with a Super Wings. Once you're Number One, you'll easily qualify for the Trag 7 power unit and some of the other very special units."

Daniel looked at the golden Super Wings and all the shiny gadgets. Some of the gadgets looked very expensive and electronic. Others were coated in shiny chrome. They all looked interesting to a curious boy like Daniel. He wondered how they worked.

"You mean a Super Wings will fly like a Spirit Flyer?"

"A Super Wings will fly *better* than a Spirit Flyer and do a whole lot more," the old woman whispered. "You just got a taste of what they can do. But you have to have an activated number card to get them to work properly. That's why it's important that you play by the rules. You've got to get into the game. Right now, your old Spirit Flyer is keeping you on the bench, so to speak. You aren't going anywhere with that old junkheap bike and I think you know it. Your mother certainly knows how to play the game. I wouldn't think you'd want to keep disappointing her the way you have by being Rank Blank. If you keep it up, you might even threaten her job at the factory. You wouldn't want that to happen."

"You mean she could lose her job because I'm Rank Blank?" Daniel asked. He felt a wave of fear pass through him. A sudden jolt of pain bit down onto the back of his neck.

"How do you think it looks if the son of an important Goliath employee refuses to use good Goliath products like a Super Wings bicycle?"

"But I am riding it," Daniel said defensively. "I ride it more than I ride my Spirit Flyer even."

"Maybe you've been riding it more lately, but that's not the point," the old woman said carefully. "Goliath Industries wants to know which bike you intend to ride the *rest of your life*. Are you loyal to their products and point of view or not? Your mother may be working for

Goliath for a very long time. You don't want to mess up."

Daniel was quiet. Even though he knew he was riding the Super Wings more, he still hoped deep down in his heart that a time would come when it would be easier to ride the Spirit Flyer. That was his wish, yet he could see that it wasn't going to be so easy. He felt an incredible pressure above his eyes, like a headache was coming on him.

"But she doesn't have to lose her job," Daniel protested feebly.

"Times are hard in this town," Mrs. Happy whispered. "Your mother knows who butters the bread. Isn't it time you learned? And look at all you will gain if you just cooperate and show a little appreciation. You'll be Number One. And with a smart boy like you, there's no telling how many Levels up you can go."

"There are more levels that two in the Point System?" Daniel asked. "How high do they go?"

"How high can you count?" the old woman asked with a giggle. "It's that many, plus one more. You can never reach the end of your potential with the Point System."

Daniel felt a great heaviness on him. All he wanted was to run away.

"You can't run away," Mrs. Happy answered his thoughts. "You can't run away from the Point System. As I've been trying to tell you, it's the only game in town. And it's the only game in the whole world!"

"Then what do I have to do?" Daniel finally blurted out. The old woman smiled. She pulled out a piece of paper from her carpetbag which looked like a sort of form.

"Just sign this paper," the old woman said.

"What is it?" Daniel asked. His eyes were wet and blurry.

"It's just a loyalty form. Basically, all it says is that as the son of a Goliath employee, you agree to ride Goliath bicycles and use Goliath products."

"What about my Spirit Flyer?" Daniel asked.

"This says you just agree not to ride it until the month is out. It's just a minor "no use" clause. Then, when we're satisfied you intend to keep your word, next month we'll have another form and a special bicycle chain and lock. Once that's taken care of, we'll discuss how you can obtain some of the fine attachments that make the Super Wings so very special. Like the Trag 7 power unit box."

"Where do I sign?" Daniel asked with a sigh.

The old woman pulled a shiny needle from her hand. Daniel's eyes went wide with fear. But before he knew it, she had grabbed his right hand and pricked his thumb. The old woman licked her lips as a little spot of blood appeared.

"Just press right there," the old woman said. She guided Daniel's hand onto the paper. A wet red thumbprint was left to dry at the bottom of the page.

"Will my number card work now?" Daniel asked.

"Not quite," the old woman said. "This is just the paperwork. You still need to prove yourself worthy. However, if you pass your initiation test into the Cobra Club, that will satisfy all the other requirements . . . at least for this month."

"But I don't know what the initiation test is yet."

Mrs. Happy just smiled and took Daniel's arm to guide him to the front door. She turned the lock and opened the door quickly. She pushed Daniel outside. "Just play the game like you mean it. Your points will be accumulating on the Big Board. You'll get the credit you so richly deserve."

The old woman smiled and then closed the door in his face. Daniel looked down at his thumb. The blood had dried already.

LOSING AND WINNING A FIGHT

16

The remaining two weeks before the big superstar tournament seemed to last an eternity for Daniel. Though he tried to tell his family and friends that he would get a real rank soon, no one seemed to believe him. And he wasn't really sure of it himself. Nothing seemed certain to him since the moment he had traveled through the Big Board. He found himself worrying about the Point System much of the time. Since getting a rank depended on him passing the Cobra Club initiation test, Daniel worried about that too.

Like all the other kids in town, Barry and the boys on the team worried about making Superstar status. The Rockets won all their games, but the final team they would play, the Wildcats, were also undefeated.

Every game was filled with the same war cries: Smash him! Blast him! Kill him! Get the ball. Score, score, score!!! Every player was just trying to survive.

Barry was already bragging about where he would put the Superstar trophy in his room. Daniel asked the President of the Cobra Club how he could be so sure, but Barry would only smile. Barry was also the only one who seemed to think Daniel would soon be rid of his Rank Blank status.

Ever since the bank had closed, most people in Centerville had grown more worried too. Doug Barn's whole family had moved away from town because Doug's parents had both lost their jobs. The same thing was happening to many other families.

In the middle of all the change and turmoil, people wanted to know where they stood. The Big Board down in Mrs. Happy's store became a regular gathering place. Within just three weeks, it seemed as if the mysterious Big Board had always been there, adding and subtracting points like a computerized fortune-telling machine. Though people often complained about losing points, fewer and fewer people complained about the Big Board itself. The concerned group of parents that had come to Mrs. Happy that first week dwindled in size. Sheriff Kramar continued to express his displeasure about the Big Board, but most of the other parents got in line and just encouraged their children to try harder to measure up.

The Big Board out at the factory only increased the power of the Point System in town. Though adults were graded on an adult Level One, the bigger Big Board worked essentially the same way. In fact, those adults in town who didn't work at the factory began to feel left out since they didn't have number cards and a rank in the overall picture. Some of the more successful business people really wished that they could compare ranks down at the barber shop and the beauty parlor like the factory workers did. Near the end of August, the town council began talking with a representative of Goliath Industries about how they could purchase various Big Boards for the rest of the people in town.

Daniel felt the pull of the Point System tugging at his own heart day in and day out. The longer he was Rank Blank, the more desperate he was to see his name in lights on the Big Board like all the other children.

Being on the outside of the Point System wore him down. If he could have talked with Susan or John Kramar, he might not have felt so isolated. But they were still out of town, and it seemed like they had been gone an eternity. He began to wonder if they were ever coming back. And even if they did come back, he wasn't sure he wanted them for his friends.

Who you had as friends was an important category in the Point Breakdown sheet. If you had friends with a good rank, you were credited more points yourself. So everyone wanted Top One Hundred kids as their friends. But the higher numbered kids tried to stick with the other higher numbers. And on down the line it went. The children divided the town into general classifications: The Big Ten, Top Hundred, the Mids (numbers two hundred through three hundred), the So-sos (three hundred through four hundred) and the Low Balls (the five and six hundreds).

Then there were the oddballs like Daniel who were Rank Blank. Though no one was sure, the word had spread around town that the Kramar children were all Rank Blanks too, but they had never even been to the Big Board to have it confirmed. Daniel felt sure they would be Rank Blank just like him since they all rode Spirit Flyers. Though he thought of Susan almost every day, he wondered if things would ever work out. He felt that if he hung out with other Rank Blank kids, he himself would be considered a Rank Blank forever. The more he thought about that, the more desperate he became to break into the Point System.

Daniel's attitude about the Spirit Flyer began to change too. Ever since he had signed the loyalty form at Mrs. Happy's store, he wished for the dreamlike Number One status he had seen when he rode through the

Big Board on the Super Wings. The more he rode the Super Wings, the less he remembered the good times he used to have riding the Spirit Flyer. After three weeks, he didn't miss the old bicycle much at all. In fact, he had begun to even resent the old bike.

He was out in the garage one morning, staring at the Spirit Flyer. It was on a Thursday, the last week of August, the day before the Super Summer Party. Barry and the other boys were planning to come over. Daniel was excited because Barry was finally going to give him the rules for passing his initiation test.

Daniel hoped they wouldn't talk about the Spirit Flyer. The last several times they had come to his house they had said a lot of mean things about the old bike. Daniel had become sensitive about even letting them in the garage anymore. In fact, he had taken an old blanket and covered the Spirit Flyer to make it less noticeable. The old bicycle was beginning to be just an embarrassment to the boy, just like his limping leg.

"I can't do much about my leg," Daniel said out loud to himself. "But I don't guess I really need two bicycles. I can only ride one anyway. Besides, I would have had a rank on the Big Board a long time ago if it wasn't for you. Everyone likes my Super Wings bike, but no one likes a junk-heap bike."

The old Spirit Flyer sat quietly on its big balloon tires. Daniel pulled the blanket back down over it. He took the plastic number card out of his pocket. He stared down at the reflected image within the card. The image began to grin up at Daniel. Then, for a moment, Daniel thought he heard a voice. The lips on his reflection were moving.

"Just admit it," the face in the card said and then giggled. "You hate the Spirit Flyer and you want to get rid of it. You'll never be accepted by any of the other kids as long as you have that junk-heap bicycle. It doesn't matter what rank you are."

"You're probably right," Daniel agreed with himself. He felt a tremendous heaviness on his neck and shoulders. Then he saw the chain in

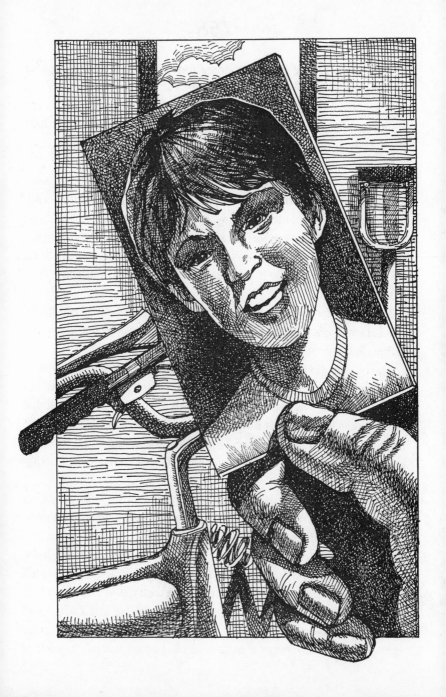

the reflection on the card. The mysterious chain didn't even surprise him anymore.

"The chain hurts," the reflection said. "But that's because you're resisting it. You're like a dog pulling on a leash. But it wouldn't hurt if you went where the chain wanted you to go."

"That makes sense," Daniel said to himself, then sighed.

"That junk-heap bicycle is pulling you down," his reflection said. "Your mother knows that. Your friends know that. The Big Board knows it and even the whole town knows it. You're the only dummy left. So why don't you get back in the game? Get rid of the Spirit Flyer. Everyone thinks you're an oddball enough as it is. Pretty soon everyone will think you are a regular fanatic if you keep that old bike. Think about that, Stupid."

And with those words, the reflection of Daniel's face froze into silence. Daniel put the card back into his pocket. That's when he saw the Cobra Club coming up the street.

The boys in the Cobra Club were yelling as they rode up into Daniel's driveway. A new boy had been asked to join since Doug Barns had left town. His name was Jason Miller. Daniel didn't really like Jason all that much because Jason was always wanting to pick a fight. Daniel just thought he was trying to prove himself. He was going to be included in the same initiation test as Daniel. Neither boy liked the idea of having to depend on the other.

Jason had even complained out loud in front of Daniel. "Why do I have to get stuck with this cripple?" Jason had said. "What if we need to run or something? I like to work alone."

Daniel had gotten red in the face. He had been ready to sail into Jason with both fists but didn't. Then he felt ashamed because he could tell the other boys in the club had wanted to see their newest two members fight it out. Jason was a little bit bigger than Daniel. He was also a rough boy with a bad temper. He had large dirty hands and a wild look in his eyes. His hair was always a mess and his clothes weren't as nice as

Daniel's clothes. Daniel was afraid of him. Ever since that day, Daniel had just tried to stay out of Jason's way. But he wondered if that would be possible if they had to go out together on the initiation test.

"Tonight is the big night," Barry said with a smile. The President of the Cobra Club was holding a large grocery sack under one arm.

"What do I have to do?" Jason demanded as he hopped off his bike. He totally ignored Daniel.

"Both you and Daniel have to work as a team on this one," Barry said.

"That's really great," Jason fumed. "I told you I can handle it by myself."

"It will be better for everyone if you do it together," Barry said. "In fact, I'll be going along to keep watch."

The boys crowded up in a small circle as Barry opened the large shopping bag. There were two rolls of toilet paper, a can of shaving cream and a plain paper sack about the size of a ten-pound bag of flour.

"What's the mission?" Jason asked. He didn't seem too impressed with the items Barry was showing them.

"We may not be invited to the Top One Hundred party that Craig and Cindy are giving tomorrow, but I still plan to attend it, one night early." The President of the Cobra Club smiled. "In fact, I plan to help them decorate to show my appreciation. And after we're through decorating, they might not even want to have a party."

"With that junk?" Jason asked. "You can't do much with a couple rolls of toilet paper and shaving cream. You need some spray paint or stuff like that."

"What's in the sack?" Daniel asked, looking at the mystery package. He figured that must be Barry's secret weapon.

"That's for me to know and you to find out tomorrow," Barry said. "Are you in or not?"

"I'm in," Jason said immediately. "But I can handle it by myself. I don't need some limp-leg creep slowing me down all night."

Daniel felt himself turning red. The boys in the club looked eagerly back and forth between the two opponents, hoping for a fight. Jason looked at Daniel with disgust.

"You both are going," Barry said. "We may need to spread the credit around on this one."

"It's your club," Jason sniffed. "When are we supposed to get there?"

"We'll meet at midnight at the edge of the town park, right there by the entrance into the pool parking lot."

"Midnight?" Daniel asked. "I'm not sure I can get out of the house that time of night."

"You either be there or you fail the test," Barry snapped impatiently.

"What if the little baby can't get out of his house?" Jason taunted. "I told you it was a mistake to bring him."

Daniel felt a wave of heat and anger rush over himself. Jason stood up and stretched. Daniel stood and faced him.

"So the cripple wants to fight me?" Jason asked. "You better get your little sister for help."

"I'm warning you," Daniel said. "Watch what you say around me."

Jason smiled at the other boys. Daniel took a step closer. His hands were in fists. Jason looked at the other boys and then turned to Daniel. And as he turned, he spat right into Daniel's face.

Daniel cried out as he lunged forward. In a second, both boys were rolling on the front lawn, clawing and punching at each other. Jason was laughing, which only made Daniel more angry. The other boys cheered them on. Only Barry watched without speaking.

Daniel took most of the blows at first. But when he tasted blood on his lip, something seemed to come over him. All the pent-up rage and shame that he had taken since the accident seemed to explode. Daniel's arms began flailing like a windmill in a tornado. Soon he was on top of Jason. He just kept hitting and hitting. His eyes were filled with tears. He could hardly see what he was hitting, but he could tell by the cries that Jason was hurting.

Daniel was still swinging when the boys in the club grabbed his arms.

It took two boys for each arm to keep Daniel from landing another blow. Jason was crawling on the ground, trying to get away. Both his lips and nose were bleeding. Grass stuck in his dirty hair and his eyes were full of fear as he looked at Daniel.

"Did you see that?" Alvin whispered. The younger boy with the big nose looked at Daniel with awe and a new respect. Daniel's chest was rising and falling as he tried to catch his breath.

"He would have killed me," Jason blubbered out. "He fights like a crazy man. It ain't fair."

"He made you look like a wimp," Jimmy commented and spat on the ground. Jason looked down, wiping the blood from his nose.

"Way to go, Danny," Barry said and patted Daniel on the back. "You'll get credit on the Big Board for sure, winning a fight like that."

Daniel stared over at Jason. Then he began brushing off his clothes. He felt like an animal. Part of him wanted to feel good for winning the fight, but he only felt sick inside. He knew you were supposed to feel brave and glorious, but he just felt worse.

"I better go," Daniel said.

"Sure thing," Barry said.

"You really nailed him," Jimmy added. "Did you guys see that?"

The other boys began to laugh. The tension was gone from the air, but it wasn't gone from Daniel's stomach. He held his side, trying to hold it all under control.

"You'll still be there tonight, won't you?" Barry asked Daniel.

"I'll be there," Daniel replied. And he knew he would. The boys were still talking as he walked back through the garage. As he closed the big garage door, Daniel saw the blanket over his Spirit Flyer. He looked sadly over at the old bicycle. Everything was sick and confused inside him. For a moment, all he wished for was to leap on the seat of the old red bicycle and fly away into the clouds. But the thoughts of the loyalty form he had signed came rushing back in.

Daniel turned away from the bike and limped into the house.

NUMBER
ONE
· · · · · · · · ·
17

That night Daniel rode through the dark streets of Centerville avoiding every street light. Though one part of him felt excited to finally be doing his initiation test, another part of him was scared stiff. His mother thought he was home asleep in his bed.

Barry and the new boy, Jason, were waiting at the edge of the town park. Jason nodded at Daniel and looked down.

"Sorry about calling you all those names," Jason said. "I guess I was wrong about you."

"That's ok," Daniel said. He didn't even want to think about the fight. He had taken a nap that afternoon, trying to forget the anger that had come spilling out. The tension and rage inside himself had scared Daniel. So he had pushed it out of his mind, thinking only about the initiation test.

Jason was carrying the brown paper bag. Daniel was glad that he didn't have to carry the shaving cream and toilet paper and the mystery package.

"Ready to go?" Barry asked with a sneaky grin.

"You bet," Jason said. He held up the bag.

"Are you sure there's no one that comes around, like a night watchman or anything?" Daniel asked.

"Are you kidding?" Barry asked. "There's nothing to watch at the town pool. Let's go."

The boys took off on their bikes. Daniel brought up the rear while Jason and Barry rode side by side whispering. When they got to the pool and clubhouse, they laid their bikes down. The night grass was already soaked wet with dew.

"Come on," Barry whispered.

The boys ran bent over toward the chain-link fence that surrounded the pool. Off in the distance, a dog was barking and barking. They stopped at the fence. Daniel thought it looked awfully high.

"I'll help you guys over," Barry said. He gripped his hands together. Jason put the bag down, stepped into Barry's hands and lunged for the top of the fence. He stayed at the top while Barry handed him the package. Then Jason dropped down to the other side. Daniel took a deep breath and did the same thing. Daniel picked up the brown paper sack that Jason had dropped when he jumped over. He was surprised by the weight.

"This seems awful heavy," Daniel said. He looked in the sack. There were still two rolls of toilet paper and a can of shaving cream. The other mystery sack was the heavy thing. "What's in this bag?"

"That's the ultimate decoration," Barry whispered. "Jason knows what to do with it. Now get going."

Daniel took a roll of toilet paper and strung it over the fence while Jason took a roll and put it on the diving board and other places. When they were finished with that, they wrote on the sidewalk with the shaving cream.

"All this so I won't be Rank Blank," Daniel muttered to himself. But he went along. He was relieved when the can of shaving cream emptied out.

That's when Jason got the paper sack that looked like a bag of flour.

"Put it down on the deep end," Barry instructed from the other side of the fence. "That's where the main pool filter outlet is located. It will spread it out from there."

"Spread what out?" Daniel asked.

"Just shut up and get over the fence," Barry commanded. Daniel did as he was told. He climbed carefully over the side of the fence and dropped back down. Jason ran over to the other boys and climbed over the fence much faster than Daniel.

Soon all three were on their bikes, pedaling as fast as they could. When they got to the town square, Daniel split off to ride home.

"Meet at my house tomorrow morning," Barry called out softly. Daniel nodded.

He rode home and left his bike in the back yard. Then he climbed back up the tree and went inside his open window. He heard the clock downstairs strike one. Soon he was fast asleep.

Daniel ate breakfast without saying much that Friday morning. He left the house on his Goliath Super Wings soon after his mother went to work. He wanted to ride by the park and pool but rode instead toward Barry's house.

Six bicycles were parked on Barry's front lawn when Daniel rode up. He hopped off his bike. Just then Barry Smedlowe opened the garage door. He smiled at Daniel.

"Danny, you're in the club all the way," Barry said. "You passed the test with flying colors. The pool decorations are fantastic. Jimmy rode by there this morning. It's the biggest, pinkest bubble bath in town."

"What?" Daniel asked. His heart began to race. "But I never—"

"You should see it, Red," Jimmy said with a big grin. "It looks like a great big sink full of pink soapsuds. They must be three-feet thick."

"Let's go," Barry said. "Seeing is believing. By now, it won't be suspicious if we ride our bikes over there. My party is going to be a huge success tonight. They'll never fix the pool up in time for that stupid Craig and Cindy."

The boys yelled in glee and hopped on their bicycles. Daniel was the last to get on his bike. As he followed the pack his mind was racing with a thousand thoughts. The boys began talking excitedly as they got near the Centerville Park.

A police car was parked by the pool and Daniel felt his heart sink. Then he saw the suds. There were great pink clouds of suds where the pool was supposed to be. The Cobra Club rode straight up to the chain-link fence which surrounded the pool. Probably fifty or more children had come to see the sight. No one even seemed to notice the strings of toilet paper and shaving cream spattered about here and there.

"Will you look at that?" Barry whispered, folding his arms across his chest. "That's been my most brilliant plan to date. "

"That's even better than the time you wrote on the school walls with the spray paint," Alvin grunted.

"You shut your mouth," Barry warned. Then he winked at Daniel. "That was a successful operation too. But nothing like this."

Sheriff Kramar was inside the pool area, talking to the pool manager, Mrs. Wagstaff. She was motioning to the pool and her face was clearly quite upset. She had a dark brown, pulpy-looking mess in her hands. Daniel realized that she was probably holding the remains of the brown paper sack that Jason had dumped in the pool.

Barry walked toward the front gate. The other boys followed. A hastily scratched sign was already posted on the bulletin board: "Pool Closed due to vandalism. No party tonight."

"Isn't that a shame," Barry said to the other boys. He winked at Daniel. "Of course, there will be a pool party tonight at my house. At least for those kids in the top two hundred."

"Here comes the sheriff, we better beat it," Doug said.

"What for?" Barry asked. "He doesn't have any proof it was us. And no one is going to squeal."

Daniel watched the sheriff coming. He opened the pool gate and then closed it. He looked at Barry and the other boys, then walked on through the crowd of children to his car. He seemed sad, Daniel thought. He wondered what Susan thought, or if she even knew about the pool yet.

With the sheriff's car gone, the excitement had died down. You could only look at a big pile of soapsuds so long.

"This place is a bore," Barry announced. "Let's get out of here."

As they rode away, the other members in the club kidded Daniel and Jason about what a great job they had done. Daniel wasn't sure what to say. Barry led the boys to the toy store. He opened the door and went in. Daniel brought up the rear.

"I've got a customer," Barry said to Mrs. Happy. He took Daniel by the arm and brought him over to the Big Board. "I told Daniel we would stop him from being Rank Blank and I meant it."

"Going to give the Big Board another try, are you?" the old woman asked and winked. Daniel pulled his number card out of his pocket. He slipped it into the slot.

"I'll buy," Barry said and got a quarter out of his pocket. He dropped it into the money slot and waited. "Go ahead and say it, Red."

"Big Board, Big Board, on the wall, how do I rank among them all?" Daniel said in a weak voice. The Big Board flashed into action, spewing numbers and letters in bright purple lights. The bell rang twice as the words froze in the darkness.

****

Daniel Bayley: Level: 2   Rank: 1   Score: 1003 points
CONGRATULATIONS TO THE NEW NUMBER ONE!!!

****

"Daniel's Number One," Jimmy Roundhouse said in surprise.

"Yeah, and he's on Level Two," Alvin added. "No one else in town is on Level Two, are they?"

Barry Smedlowe's mouth dropped open as he read the listing over again.

"He can't be Number One. I'm Number One," Barry blurted out. The President of the Cobra Club looked at Mrs. Happy.

"Well, the Big Board giveth and the Big Board taketh away," Mrs. Happy said with a sigh.

"But it can't do that!" Barry replied. The owner of the toy store wasn't listening to him though.

"Congratulations, my boy," the old woman said and pinched Daniel's cheek. "To go from Rank Blank to Number One is quite an achievement. Quite an achievement indeed."

"But how can that be?" Barry demanded. He looked at Daniel and frowned.

"He's on Level Two," the old woman said simply. "Anyone on Level Two is ahead of those people on Level One. Didn't I tell you that?"

"But how can he be on Level Two?" Barry asked.

"I imagine it's because he has a Goliath Super Wings bicycle," the old woman said. "Like I've been telling you. They are very special, powerful bikes. Besides, Daniel here is a very smart, capable boy. He's also quite a good fighter when push comes to shove. The Big Board likes those qualities in an individual. Remember, it's survival of the fittest these days."

Daniel pulled his number card out of the Big Board. A large number one was on the card. And on the other side, the reflection of his face was wearing a big smile. Daniel looked up and saw that Barry Smedlowe wasn't smiling at all.

"We better go," Daniel said, seeing the anger on the bigger boy's face. The other boys nodded. They all went outside. As they got out on the sidewalk, they looked back inside and saw Barry arguing with the old woman. The other boys slapped Daniel on the back.

"See you at the party tonight," they said.

The news about Daniel being the new Number One spread like wildfire around the town. Cindy Meyers and Craig Banks called off their pool party just like Barry had planned. Of course, Barry hadn't planned on being knocked out of his top standing in the Point System. Even though he had only dropped back to Number Two, he fumed all day as he got ready for his party.

No one was more happy for Daniel's rise on the Point System than his mother. She had been glowing since she heard the news. "I knew we'd get things back the way they used to be," Mrs. Bayley said proudly, as she drove Daniel and Denise to Barry's house for the party that night. "My two kids are winners all the way."

"You would have thought I won a million dollars or something," Daniel muttered to himself. Daniel felt more than a little confused by his sudden rise on the Point System. Even though Mrs. Happy had told him that he would eventually get to the top rank, he never really quite believed it. On one hand he was happy to be accepted, but deep inside he knew he had betrayed a part of himself by signing the "no use" clause on his Spirit Flyer.

He was even more confused at the party. Children and other kids that had totally avoided him were now slapping him on the back and acting like they had been friends with Daniel all along. Though he liked the attention at first, Daniel wondered if they were just hoping for some of his friendship points. Many of these same children had ridiculed him the day before at soccer practice. The more compliments Daniel got, the less he liked them.

Barry was friendly to Daniel but through gritted teeth. Though Mrs. Happy had explained the situation to the President of the Cobra Club several times that morning, he found it hard to accept that owning a Goliath Super Wings qualified Daniel for a Level Two standing. The old woman had been hard to pin down exactly on how some of the finer points of the Point System actually worked. Barry finally quit arguing when he saw his own point total begin to drop before his eyes. He knew that if you complained too much, it only made things worse.

The former Number One had other things to worry about anyway. He had gathered the officers of the Cobra Club in the garage to discuss the tournament the next day. Another boy was also in the meeting. Daniel had seen the boys go into the garage. He was curious and followed them. He walked into the garage but stopped when he heard the other boys talking.

"Shouldn't Daniel be here?" Jimmy asked. "After all, things have changed since he's the new Number One."

"I don't care what the limpy-gimpy's number is," Barry snarled. "He's still not an officer. Besides, I didn't come here to talk about him. I'll get my rank back. Just you wait. In the meantime, we have to take care of tomorrow's game. That's why I brought Robert here since he's the goalie for the Wildcats."

Daniel paused and listened. He wasn't surprised they didn't invite him to the meeting. But he was curious why the boy named Robert was attending a secret meeting of the Cobra Club. "We've got to be the Superstar team," Barry said. "And Robert here has agreed to be our insurance. Just like the other guys on the other teams. He's already been paid in money and points. I'm also throwing a Combo-Gizmo into the deal just to show I'm a nice guy. But I wanted us to be sure he makes it look good, like he's not cheating."

Daniel strained his ears to catch every word. Apparently, Barry had used money from the Cobra Club treasury to pay off the goalie on the opposing team. And from what Barry hinted at, this wasn't the first time they had made this arrangement.

Daniel hid behind a shelf as Robert left. He could still hear the other boys talking. "Why are you going to give him a Combo-Gizmo too?" Jimmy asked after Robert was gone.

"Because he wouldn't make a deal without one thrown in," Barry said. "But he'll only get it after we make the Superstar team. Of course, I didn't say I would give him a Combo-Gizmo that worked. I dropped one on the sidewalk the other day. Now it's got a funny rattle inside. That's the one I'm giving to Robert."

The other boys began laughing. Daniel started to limp away. That's when he knocked a paint can off the shelf. The other boys surrounded him in an instant.

"Well if it isn't Number One trying to snoop in on a secret club officer's meeting," Barry snarled. Daniel's face turned red.

"How much did you hear, Red?" Jimmy demanded.

"Enough," Daniel said. He bent down to pick up the paint can.

"Well, you might as well know anyway," Barry replied. "You're already in on the pool stuff. Just keep your mouth shut and do as I say. We'll make the Superstar team, get the free prizes, not to mention the free memberships out at the country club. Danny boy wants the same thing we want, don't you?"

"Sure," Daniel said without much enthusiasm.

"I thought so," Barry replied. "Let's get back to the party. Just remember, after the tournament we'll have a party no one will forget."

The boys all shouted and howled and ran back inside the house. Daniel stood by the garage. He took the number card out of his pocket and stared at it quietly.

"You've got it made now," the reflected face said softly. "By tomorrow night you'll be the Superstar of your dreams!"

DANIEL
ROBOT
BAYLEY

• • • • • • • •

18

The Super Summer Party was a big success. Since school was going to start the next Tuesday, everyone was trying to end the summer by having as much fun as possible.

Saturday morning came with the excitement that the Goliath Sports League Tournament had arrived at last. The play-off games would be that morning. And that evening the awards ceremony and cookout would take place. After eating a dinner of hamburgers and hot dogs and lemonade, the Superstar teams would be recognized. Trophies and prizes would be handed out to each player on those teams, courtesy of Goliath Industries.

More than anything, Daniel wished he were sick that Saturday morning. He almost wished he were stuck in his old wheelchair because then he could just sit out the whole mess and no one would care. Daniel groaned. Even without the wheelchair, he almost felt paralyzed from the people and things that kept pulling him in opposite directions. He got out of bed slowly and sighed as he walked toward the upstairs bathroom.

Having a rank, especially a coveted rank like the top position on the Point System, wasn't anything like the boy had imagined it would be. No matter how hard he tried, he knew something was wrong deep inside himself. All during the party he couldn't stop thinking about what the Cobra Club had done to the pool and what they were going to do that day in the big tournament game. Daniel wanted to just climb back in bed and sleep so he wouldn't have to think about it.

Denise was already dressed and pressed in her clean jersey. She was stationed in front of the bathroom mirror, anxiously trying to hide any blemish or spot on her face that might cause her to lose points. She had the latest copy of *Pretty You* magazine propped up on the sink. A picture of a perfect face was staring up out of the pages. Denise was looking at the face, then trying to add make-up in just the right places so her own face would be perfect too. Daniel watched her without speaking. Then he went downstairs.

His mother was drinking coffee. She urged him to hurry and get ready. She didn't want them to be late. You could lose points for being late for an important date. Daniel did as he was told, though not as fast as his mother wanted.

He ate breakfast by himself and then got dressed. He absolutely hated putting on the uniform of the Rockets. He felt as if they were prison clothes. As he put on his long white-and-blue socks, he rubbed the ugly red-and-purple scars at the bottom of his right leg. His leg was aching and sore, but not so sore that he couldn't play in the game. He tied the laces of his shoes tightly, took a deep breath, then stood and walked out of his room as if he were going to his doom.

His mother wanted to drive him to the athletic field where the tournament was being held. Denise was already in the car. Daniel wanted to ride his bike. He stood beside the car door arguing with his sister and mother.

"But you'll get sweaty and stinky if you ride your bike," Denise complained. "I just don't think it's a good idea. I've heard of several kids who have lost points because of sweating too much. You're not supposed to let people see you sweat, according to some rules."

"Oh, dry up," Daniel said. "Everyone sweats when it's hot or when they play hard."

"But this is *before* the game," Denise said primly. "You may not care about how you look, but I do. And since you're my brother, it doesn't seem fair to me for you to act the way you do. You're Number One now and you have to act a little different when you're in such a good position."

"I think Denise has a point, Dan," Mrs. Bayley said. "A little sweat at the wrong time can be embarrassing. And you need to develop a strategy to protect that top rank. A lot of children would like to be in your position."

Daniel started to protest, but then he stopped. For an instant he felt a twinge of fear that someone would take away his high position. He realized how much he did care deep down about his rank.

"You may not care about yourself, but at least you could consider Denise in all of this," his mother said. Daniel felt a painful tug at every word.

"I promise I will pedal slow enough so I won't sweat," Daniel said. His mother and Denise looked at him with doubtful eyes and sighed. Then his mother started the car and pulled out of the driveway.

Daniel went back inside the house and slowly walked up to his room. His number card was on his dresser. He looked at the big Number One. Then, without knowing why, Daniel went to his closet and got out the wooden milk box with his most secret possessions. He opened the combination lock and lifted the lid. The Spirit Flyer Vision goggles were lying on top of his copy of *The Book of the Kings*. Daniel picked up both items.

"I wish I knew what to do," Daniel said and sighed. He opened the old book and flipped through the pages. Several pages had been marked with an ink pen. Daniel looked down at one story. It was about the Kingson and the time he had been tempted to become a traitor by Treason, the enemy. Treason offered the whole world as a reward if the Kingson would bow down to Treason. Only the Kingson refused.

Daniel closed the book sadly. He was going to put the things away when he looked at the goggles. In a flash, he took the goggles and number card and ran to the bathroom. He stood before the full-length mirror on the back of the bathroom door. He took a deep breath, closed his eyes and slipped on the goggles.

"Please let me see what I need to see," Daniel wished to the Kings. Then he opened his eyes. At first he wanted to scream, but he was paralyzed with fear. In the mirror, around his head, was a swarm of black shadowy snakes. They seemed to just cover his shoulders, feasting and biting. There was also a host of the leechlike serpents wrapped around the bottom of his short right leg. Daniel stared in silent horror at the reflection of himself. For the first time in a long time he suddenly realized that he was dying deep inside, that the snakes were slowly draining the life from his body.

There was a light that seemed to be coming out of his chest from his heart. But the light was mostly hidden by the snakes and the heavy chain. Daniel stared at the glimpses of light and felt a faint hope. Instantly, the light seemed brighter. Something about the light seemed very different, as if it were special or expensive. Daniel couldn't decide until he remembered a movie he had seen about some kings. The kings wore crowns of gold so bright, the light they reflected almost seemed like royal light. That's what this light seemed like to the boy—royal light.

But if it was royal light, it was drowning in the darkness of the squirm-

ing snakes. Daniel felt a great heaviness inside as he stared at himself. For the first time he was willing to admit to himself that he had allowed this to happen, that by making a deal with Mrs. Happy and going along with the Cobra Club initiation test, he had somehow sold himself back into the slavery of the chain.

At that moment, the great chain stretched tight. Daniel shuddered as he saw the chain going straight down into his hand, disappearing into the darkness of the number card. The chain tugged and tugged again as Daniel heard laughter coming from the number card. That's when he couldn't look anymore. He pulled off the goggles.

He went to his room. He threw the goggles on the bed. For a moment, Daniel thought he would just explode. He was being pulled in so many directions, he felt as if he would be pulled apart. He wanted to cry, but then remembered he could lose points if someone saw him crying. They would think he was a sissy because big boys weren't supposed to cry. That was a rule in the Point System.

Daniel felt as if he were a prisoner to so many things, things you couldn't see or fight back against. He didn't think it was fair. For the first time he truly realized why it was called the ghostslave—you couldn't grab that person because he was out of reach deep inside you. The boy sighed and put the number card in his pocket as he went back downstairs. "You can't fight it," he said in deep discouragement. He got on his Super Wings bicycle. "You can't fight something you can't see, and there's no way to win anyhow. You end up Rank Blank. An outsider and an oddball."

Daniel rode to the field, feeling dead inside. He pedaled the bicycle mechanically, just like a robot. That's what he decided he was, a kind of human robot, following a dotted line of points. He pedaled down the middle of the street, right on top of the painted dotted line that led all the way to the Centerville school grounds.

The tournament field was a place of celebration. Banners and bright balloons flew in the air. Many voices were blaring out instructions from the loudspeakers attached to telephone poles. Everywhere you looked were children in uniforms, prancing and moving as if they were anxious springs ready to shoot into space.

Daniel leaned against a pole. He saw the Rockets gathered together at the end of the field. He walked over slowly, his limp seeming more painful at every step. He joined his team members and did what he was supposed to do to warm up. Daniel Robot Bayley. He would just act, he bitterly told himself. He was a slave. The ghost inside had won. His mother and sister had won. The Cobra Club had won. Mrs. Happy had won. The Point System had won. He had won the top rank, but he was beaten.

Not only had the Point System won, but so did the Rockets. Barry scored three goals. The goalie had just missed the ball each time. Daniel knew why. He stopped more goal attempts once the Rockets were safely ahead, but Daniel knew. When the whistles blew and the game was over, Daniel jumped up and cheered like the other boys, but it was the robot that jumped, not Daniel.

"We did it, Red," Barry shouted, dancing around. "We're the Super-stars now. All the way! I can't wait to see the prizes we get. I hope we get some cash. I'm saving up to buy a Goliath Super Wings. Mrs. Happy says she may be getting some in the store soon."

Daniel was surprised by the news. Though he hated to admit it, he wondered if Barry would get to be Number One again if he had a Super Wings bicycle too. For an instant, Daniel felt a tug of fear deep inside. He remembered too well the days and weeks of being Rank Blank.

"I may be getting some good attachments for my Super Wings," Daniel told Barry. "Mrs. Happy told me about them."

"Really?" Barry asked. Daniel could tell that the President of the Cobra Club looked worried. Somehow, that made Daniel feel better inside. But before Barry could worry long, he got some good news. He was selected as Most Valuable Player for the game because of his three goals. And as the coaches counted up the statistics, it also turned out that Barry had scored the most goals during the whole sports league season. Daniel wondered how much each goal had cost in money and points.

The boys were shouting and laughing and slapping each other on the back. Coach Goober was smiling and scratching his hairy chest and legs.

"We won! We won!" the boys all began to shout at once. "We won! We won!" Daniel joined in the chorus of the victory shout, but he couldn't continue. He tried to cheer, then a wave of guilt came over the boy. He knew the team had cheated. And he still felt bad about the mess he had helped create at the pool. Every part of his body screamed out, "Foul! Foul!" He knew the boys hadn't won at all. They were just like him, slaves and robots, mere puppets attached by their chains to the Big Board. None of them had won a thing. The real Official winner of the summer was the Point System.

While the cheering continued, Daniel slipped away from the crowd. Nothing seemed to add up anymore. He pedaled home slowly, counting his losses.

THE
MOMENT
OF GLORY
· · · · · · · ·
19

Daniel stayed in his room the rest of the day. His mother was jubilant that he was not only Number One but an official Superstar. Denise's team had won in the girls division and she was a Superstar too. And besides that, she had gone all the way up to rank number twelve in just a few hours. Mrs. Bayley had splurged and bought two Point Breakdown print-out sheets, one before and one after the game. They were still talking about it when Daniel came downstairs.

"No doubt about it, I've got two Superstar kids," Mrs. Bayley beamed.

"And that makes you a Superstar mother," Denise replied. She was still studying her second Point Breakdown sheet.

"Being the sister of the person who's Number One really helps,"

Denise said. "Look at all the points I got. It's under the Family category."

Mrs. Bayley smiled and nodded as she read the figure. "I just knew Daniel could make his good points show if he just tried hard enough. I was afraid that Rank Blank stuff would go on forever. But I knew he had it in him. Well, we better go. The award ceremony is starting up soon. We need to be on time so my superstars can collect the spoils of victory."

Though his mother wanted them to ride to the awards ceremony together as a family, Daniel refused. He rode the golden Goliath Super Wings bicycle to the athletic field alone. The place was jammed with cars and pickup trucks. He weaved through the parked cars, past fenders and tailgates.

At the field, the bleachers were already filled with people eating. The tables of food were set in front of the bleachers on the high-school track. Out on the grass was a long speaker's platform. A single microphone stood on a stand. And right behind the platform was a huge Big Board, bigger than the one in the toy store. It was raised up high, fastened between two poles. Big bright purple lights spelled out the message: *Welcome Superstars!!!*

The air seemed charged with many different feelings for the town: a certain sadness that always came with the end of another summer. The new beginnings of another school year. The feelings of being older for the children entering a new grade—and for the parents realizing that their children were growing up so fast.

But this was unlike the end of any other summer. There was an almost unspoken fear carried in every heart. In the weeks since the bank closed, the changes in the world seemed to be rushing like dark storm clouds on the horizon. People in the small town of Centerville wondered what those clouds held for them, and when or if the storm would hit their town.

Like most people, Daniel felt a sense of loss to see the summer end. The big brick school buildings loomed nearby. He looked forward to being back in school, to seeing the teachers and the books he would be reading. He felt safe in classrooms, though he didn't like the weariness and boredom that sometimes came with schoolwork. He wanted to know new ideas and master new skills, like ways to measure the volume of a sphere or the mystery of how a cell divides or the wonder of looking at a whole new world under a microscope or seeing farther into distant space with a telescope.

But all those feelings were put aside as the big field lights came on and lit up the athletic field. The crowd cheered briefly, then went back to eating. Daniel forgot everything except the ceremony ahead—the ceremony that would honor secret lies.

He saw Barry lingering around the bottom of the platform. The rest of the Cobra Club was gathered around their leader, laughing and talking. Other boys were talking to Barry too. Being chosen the most valuable player was quite an honor and Barry was enjoying every second of it. Under the bright field lights, Barry's white teeth lit up his smiles. Daniel rode out across the grass.

"We did it," Barry said with a grin. "Just like I told you."

"Yeah," Daniel said, trying to force a smile. Daniel parked his bike and got some food. He sat by himself on a metal folding chair. He ate and watched the activities around him. Some girls and boys were kicking a soccer ball behind the Big Board out in the middle of the field. The night started to get damp as the darkness fell.

Coach Carothers stepped up to the microphone and turned it on. He coughed twice, then began speaking. "Please take your places, and we'll get right on with the festivities. I'm sure these girls and boys want to get their awards sooner rather than later."

Daniel climbed up on the platform with all the other Rockets. The winning girls' team, the Cougars, sat on the other side of the platform. Barry, having been chosen as the team captain, sat next to Coach Goober. Daniel sat in the last chair on the end.

Daniel looked in the stands and found his mother sitting in the front row. Near her was Mr. Cyrus Cutright, and next to him was Mrs. Happy. She was all smiles. His mother waved at Daniel and Denise and smiled proudly. The smells of hamburgers and hot dogs and fruit pies drifted across the platform.

Coach Carothers stood at the microphone and cleared his throat. The noise in the crowd died down. "It's appropriate that we all be gathered together on the fields of competition for this celebration of character and excellence," the coach said in almost sacred tones. "The events of the last few weeks around the world haven't left us much to celebrate in many ways, other than the fact that we're still here." The people in the crowd nodded and whispered. "But thanks to Goliath Industries, we've been fortunate to hang on to the peace and the prosperity that we've all worked so hard to attain."

The crowd stood to their feet and cheered. Whistles blew, hands clapped, the Big Board flashed on and off: *Thanks Goliath!!!*

The coach turned and looked at the flashing letters. "The Big Board really just about says it all," Coach Carothers said. "Thanks, Goliath Industries. And thanks to all the swell kids and parents who've helped make the sports league a success."

More applause broke out.

"Now let's get right down to honoring the superstars." He called out the names of the winning girls team first. They each came up and got a trophy and a certificate of membership in the Goliath Country Club and a package of prize certificates from the local stores. The crowd applauded and cheered after each name was called. Daniel watched his mother clapping when it was Denise's turn to get her trophy.

Then it was the Rockets' turn to be introduced. "The Rockets are a team of real go-getters," Coach Carothers announced. "And Coach Goober has done a heck of a job in getting these boys into great shape in such a short time."

Coach Goober nodded and waved his hairy hand as the crowd clapped.

"Thanks, Coach Goober," Mr. Carothers said. "Now let's give out the trophies. It gives me great pleasure to award not only a Superstar trophy but also the Most Valuable Player award to Barry Smedlowe."

Barry stood up and swaggered to the microphone. He waved and smiled as the crowd applauded. They applauded extra loud when the Big Board flashed the message: *Barry Smedlowe: Most Valuable Player!!!*

"I'm just a player on a team of a bunch of great guys," Barry said into the microphone. "We couldn't do it alone."

"No," Daniel said to himself. "Not without the help of those guys that you paid off."

The crowd applauded madly once more as Barry sauntered back to his seat. One by one, the other boys were briefly introduced and called up to the microphone. And one by one they took their trophies and certificates for prizes. The last name announced was Daniel's. He limped carefully to the center of the tables to Coach Carothers. The coach smiled and shook Daniel's hand.

"The last member on our team is Daniel Bayley, another newcomer to Centerville," Coach said. "This boy showed a lot of spunk and courage out there. In fact, he overcame a slow start in the Point System. But in recent days, through hard work and a lot of determination, this boy has received the coveted top rank on the Big Board as the new Number One!"

The crowd cheered and applauded as the Big Board lit up with a new message: *Daniel Bayley: Number One Superstar!!!* Daniel looked over his shoulders at the flashing lights. The crowd stood to their feet, wild with cheers. Daniel saw his mother clapping hard, her eyes filled with pride and tears. This was indeed the place of his dreams. He was in, accepted by all. This was his moment of glory.

As he looked at his applauding mother, he noticed two children on the edge of the crowd, sitting on two old red bicycles. Daniel felt as if he were turning upside-down when he saw Susan Kramar looking right into his eyes. Her simple look cut through all the pomp and circumstance of the occasion. Something burned deep inside Daniel's heart.

The coach was talking and Daniel felt himself slipping away. For a moment, he was high above the clouds in a bright blue sky, holding onto the handlebars of his Spirit Flyer. The wind was on his face, and he was looking at a distant figure, a brightly lit figure, a kingly figure. That's when Daniel realized it was a King. The King's Prince himself. Daniel had never seen such a glorious sight. The boy felt weak in his knees as the light shone out to him. And not only was there light, but there was music, as if thousands of voices were singing out praises to the King's Prince. The boy's heart was deeply stirred.

The applause jarred Daniel back to the athletic field. But the applause suddenly seemed empty and plain compared to the glory the boy had just glimpsed. Coach Carothers shook his hand and asked if he had anything to say. Daniel stepped up to the microphone. The crowd paused and was suddenly quiet. Daniel looked at different faces in the crowd. His eyes went from his smiling proud mother to Mrs. Happy and to Susan and John Kramar.

Then Daniel looked inside himself. He saw the waiting King in the distance, but only for an instant. That's when the light shone so brightly in the boy's heart that he knew what he must do. He had known all along.

COUNTDOWN
TO
ZERO
· · · · · · · · ·
20

Daniel stared at the crowd. The silence became uncomfortable as everyone waited for him to say something.

"I can't accept this award," he said abruptly into the microphone. "We didn't win it fair. There was cheating on our team and with some of the Wildcats' players too. They were paid off. So I can't accept this. I'm sorry."

Daniel gave back the trophy and certificates to a stunned Coach Carothers. Suddenly a great weight lifted off his shoulders and head. At the bottom of his short right leg, he even felt something, as if a tensed muscle had relaxed.

The crowd was silent. Then people began to whisper and talk. Some began to boo. "Cheater!" somebody yelled out.

"Liar!" Barry Smedlowe stood up and yelled. His eyes were full of fear.

Coach Carothers was totally unprepared for Daniel's brief announcement. He grabbed Daniel by the shoulder. "What did you say, young man?"

"Liar!" Barry shouted. He stood and pointed at Daniel. "He's trying to ruin everything! He was the one who put soap in the town pool. He told me. Now he's trying to get us all in trouble. He even cheated in the Point System so he could be Number One. He's nothing but a troublemaker. He was Rank Blank from the beginning, and he'll always be a Rank Blank. He's just trying to cheat us honest boys and girls out of the rank we deserve."

"Yeah," the other boys on the Rockets shouted out.

"That's not true," Daniel said with surprise. He suddenly felt hot and afraid, a blush creeping over his freckled face. "I'm not trying to cheat anyone out of anything. I'm trying to be honest."

"Get him!" Barry yelled. He threw a wad of paper at Daniel that hit him in the chest.

"Get him!" someone else yelled out. "He's a point robber. A fake!"

Then, suddenly, the whole crowd seemed to go wild, as if something dark and powerful had been unleashed. It was as if all the fear about jobs, the Big Board, the Point System and a million dark secrets all came to the surface. People came out of the bleachers, confused and angry. When Daniel saw them coming toward the platform and saw the looks in their eyes, he felt a wave of panic.

Daniel pushed his way through the gathering crowd on the platform. The boys on the Rockets were on their feet coming toward him. They had blocked the set of steps down by the front, so Daniel pushed his way to the back of the platform. The other boys ran after him. Daniel jumped. He tried to hit the ground and start running all at the same time. But he slipped and fell. A sharp pain shot through his right leg.

"Get the Rank Blank," the boys shouted.

Daniel rubbed his leg as he sat in the wet grass and dirt. The boys grinned as they moved toward him. They knew he couldn't run away. Daniel wanted to cry out for help, but his cries would have been lost in the growing noise from all the confusion. He could see the adults gathering on the platform. But they were too busy arguing to look at Daniel.

The President of the Cobra Club held his fake-gold Superstar trophy, tapping it slowly in his hand like a club. Daniel had never seen such a wild look in Barry's eyes. "You're nothing but a Rank Blank spoiler," Barry spat out at Daniel.

Daniel got up and shuffled backward as the mob of boys advanced. The fear inside only kept growing as he saw the hate in their eyes. Daniel was about to turn and run when he backed into something hard. He spun around and came face to face with his own dark reflection in the Big Board. Only the face shining out was laughing. A long dark chain was wrapped around its neck. Daniel stared horrified as he saw the hands in the reflection yank on the chain. At that instant, Daniel was slammed up against the darkness of the Big Board.

Barry's eyes gleamed with hatred. Daniel struggled to free himself but his legs wouldn't move. He couldn't even see the adults anymore. The darkness grew as it seemed some of the lights had been turned off. Barry looked over his shoulder to see what the adults were doing. Then he looked back at Daniel and smiled. Daniel struggled wildly once more, but the boys all stepped closer. They spread out in a half circle, one side going to the right end of the Big Board, and the other boys closing in on the left. Now there was no escape.

"Let me go," Daniel murmured, almost in a cry. He felt ashamed of his fear, knowing the other boys could see him. But just then, he fell forward as the Big Board suddenly released it's grip.

The other boys laughed to see Daniel lying in the dirt. "Look, the crippled boy fell down," Barry said. The other boys howled.

"He needs his mommy," Alvin shouted. "Little boy fall down, go wah wah."

Daniel got to his knees. He looked at the faces of his team members. Barry was quiet. He ran his hand through his hair. Daniel started to run toward the left, hoping to break through the line of boys. But before he could take two steps, he was pulled back as if a leash were attached to the back of his neck. His feet flipped out from under him. The boys all howled with laughter again to see Daniel fall.

"Not so fast, Superstar," his reflection said. "I want you to see this." And in a flash the Big Board came to life in a sputter of electricity and purple lights. Then across the top, the familiar letters formed across the top of the dark panel:

****

THE POINT SYSTEM

****

Daniel stared fearfully at the words. In the shadow of the ominous Big Board, the boys circled around Daniel. They looked up at the flashing lights and smiled.

"They can't see me," Daniel's reflection said and laughed. "But I can see them. I want to watch the whole fight where they rip you apart, piece by piece, point by point."

The Big Board hummed into activity. Then the words appeared:

****

Daniel Bayley: Point countdown to Rank Blank. 1003 Points.

****

"A countdown!" Barry yelled, reading the words. "Mrs. Happy told me about this last week. It's great. You just say it."

"What do you mean?" Alvin asked with interest.

"You can make him a zero," Barry said. "Watch the Big Board as I talk. Daniel Bayley is a crippled, Rank Blank snitch." And at the instant he spoke the words, the point total began to subtract, losing ten points.

Daniel felt Barry's words hit like punches. The other boys looked at Daniel eagerly and then looked back at the point total.

"Daniel Bayley is a redhead Superstar spoiler," Barry yelled out. The point total on the Big Board dropped more. Daniel again tensed up as each word hit him like a stone.

His reflection in the Big Board cackled in laughter. "They'll never accept you," the reflection laughed. "I told you to keep quiet. You could have been up there with the rest of them, but no, you are a spoiler . . ."

"Daniel Bayley is a lying squealer," Alvin shouted out. "And a tattle-tale." Once again the words hit Daniel and the points dropped on the Big Board. Daniel felt weak from the blows. That was when he looked down. His eyes opened wide in surprise when he saw ghostly snakes biting down on his chest and legs and arms. But what was even more surprising were the watery names written on the backs of the leechlike serpents. One said, "Squealer." Another snake had the name, "Tattle-tale." On another it said, "Spoiler." One attached to his shorter right leg said, "Crippled." They were the very names the boys had used to insult Daniel. He was still looking down at the attached serpents when another boy shouted out.

"He's a gimpy limpy lying simpy," the boy yelled. At the same time as the boy spoke, four more of the ghostlike snakes popped into view. With an almost silent hiss, they bit down on Daniel's body as each word was said. The names were written on each snake. The "Gimpy" and "Limpy" snakes on Daniel's right leg were next to the other snake. The bites burned as if filled with poison. And then Daniel realized the snakes *were* filled with poison, only poison of a different kind. These snakes were filled with the poison of hatred and fear and blind ignorance that came out of the boys who spoke them into existence. The point total on the Big Board subtracted again as the words were spoken.

"See how it works?" Barry asked, looking at the faces of the other boys. "You just keep calling him names and his point total will drop. And when he reaches absolute zero, we'll get him!"

A shout rose up among the boys. All at once, they all began yelling out at Daniel like a crowd of fans at a boxing match. Only they were yelling things much worse. The names came so fast and loud that Daniel fell to his knees as the writhing word snakes began to cover him.

Soon the names turned to curses, and the worst sort of words the boys could imagine. The snakes feasted on Daniel. He could actually see the ghostly snakes shooting out of the mouths of his accusers as they spoke. A dark smokelike fog was also pouring out of the mouths of many of the yelling boys. Some boys were even spitting and drooling as they shouted. The lights on the Big Board flashed more brightly as Daniel's point total dropped closer to zero. Daniel felt himself growing weaker and weaker, smaller and smaller, as if he were on the verge of disappearing altogether under the crush of the snakes filled with venomous hatred. Their bodies seemed to be covering him as they gathered to feast.

He could no longer hear any of the words, he only felt them piling on, feasting on his own fear and shame. And the weaker he got, the more ashamed and afraid he felt. He felt worthless and useless, as if he deserved to be taken over by his enemies.

The point total had subtracted all the way below a hundred and was dropping fast, the digits flashing by. As Daniel saw the score rapidly falling, his own hope was disappearing. The boys shouted out in approval as the score fell below fifty, then thirty, then twenty. And as it fell to ten, they began the countdown to nothingness. Daniel's last hope was a wish and a questioned pleading to the Kings.

"Ten, nine, eight, seven, six, five, four, three, two, one . . . ZERO!!!"

Their shout ripped through the sky. Bells and buzzers blasted out of the Big Board as the new words appeared, flashing on and off.

****

Daniel Bayley: The biggest nothing in town!!!! Absolute Zero and Rank Blank.

****

Then all at once, the Big Board began to fill up with the words describing Daniel with all the names and curses and shrieks the boys had shouted. The dark panel was so quickly filled with words that they became a garbled nonsense collection of words on top of letters.

Daniel was lying on the ground in a heap, holding his hands over his head. He wept in shame before the shadow of the Big Board. "He's absolute zero now," Barry announced, holding up his Superstar trophy. "Let's get the Rank Blank and finish him off."

The mob of boys surged forward in a frenzied shout. But at that moment, the light came on. In a flash brighter than lightning, two beams of light cut the deepening darkness around the Big Board. And with that light came a crashing sound of music more lovely than any morning's sunrise. All at once, the angry mob of boys fell in a heap to the ground, crushed under by the glory passing over them, the glory that can only come from the gaze of the King.

WHAT
REALLY
COUNTS
· · · · · · · ·
21

The whole field became quiet. No one could move because the King had wished it. Everyone had fallen into the peace of the Deeper World as the Kingson's presence filled the place. The silence was vibrant and rich, the way silence often is in the Deeper World, especially before the King.

Daniel felt his head being gently lifted up. The light all around shone on his tear-stained face. In that light, Daniel felt the courage to look deeper. A great cloud of light seemed to be over the whole field. And out of the cloud of wind and light, they appeared—two old red bicycles dove down from the cloud of light. The bikes zoomed once over his head in a low-pitched hum. His eyes went wide in surprise as two sets

of fat bicycle tires slowly passed over him the second time and stopped not ten feet away.

Daniel lifted his head higher, feeling the hopes of his wishes being answered. Though the light all around him was blindingly bright, Daniel could still see the two riders' faces. Susan Kramar was looking at Daniel with great concern. John Kramar stopped in the air beside her, hovering three feet off the ground.

"What do you think?" John asked Susan.

"There's still time," Susan said. "I believe the Kingson can change anything."

She looked down on Daniel and frowned. The ghostly snakes that had gathered to feast on the boy's fears and shame had all disintegrated the instant the glorious light hit them. Yet they left a stinking odor and a black, tarry slime which oozed off of Daniel in stringy globs. Trying not to notice it, she hopped off her old red bicycle and took Daniel's hand.

Daniel sat up. When he saw the slimy stuff on himself, he felt ashamed once more to be seen by Susan and John. And at the moment of his shame, the Big Board, which had been frozen, went into a frenzy of action. A new message appeared as Susan helped Daniel to his feet. The message blinked on and off in big purple letters.

****

Daniel Bayley: A pointless fool and failure to himself, his friends and the Three Kings.

****

Daniel stared at the message and felt horrified and exposed. That's when the message started to grow bigger. The letters got taller and taller and blinked on and off, on and off.

"It's true," Daniel said in shame as he looked at the message. "I can't do anything right."

As he stared at the Big Board, he cringed when he saw a figure in the deep darkness that seemed to be moving closer and closer. Daniel knew without looking it was the reflection of himself. The ghostslave ran up to the very edge of the Big Board and seemed larger than life. "You're mine," the ghostslave said. Then he looked at Susan and John. He sneered at them. "You're too late. He's reached zero. I've got him."

"It's not true!" Susan said to the ghostslave. Then she turned to Daniel. "He's a liar, Daniel. But you still have to face your fears. You can't let things from the past or the Point System make you a slave the rest of your life. The ghostslave can make you believe he owns you, that he holds you on the chain, like a dog on a leash."

"But I've lied and cheated and done awful things, things I don't even want to talk about," Daniel said. "And it was all so I could get a better rank in the Point System. I didn't want to care about being Rank Blank, but I do care. I used to be popular. Before my accident, people used to like me a lot."

"There's nothing wrong with people liking you," Susan said sympathetically. "But they don't have to control you. You don't have to wear a false face or pretend or cheat to get people to like you. Even if they did end up liking you, they wouldn't really like you at all, but a person you've pretended to be. That's the ghostslave trying to take you over again. He's the one who will lie and cheat and do anything to be liked and popular. He's the one who's sold out to the Point System. Don't you see? He's trying to drag you from the Kingdom of the Kings back into his world."

"But what other world is there?" Daniel asked. "I have to live in Centerville. I have to live with my mother and my friends."

"You still belong to the Kingdom of the Three Kings," Susan said. "And in their Kingdom, you aren't measured by points, but by love and mercy and forgiveness."

Susan's words went straight to his heart. But then he saw the black slime oozing off his body. The old fears came back. "But look at me," Daniel moaned. "I am a mess, an absolute zero."

"That's not true," Susan said. "The Kings love you and that's what counts. In *The Book of the Kings* it says that real love doesn't count up wrongs, but hopes all things. When someone loves you, they aren't loving your good and bad points, they love you for just being you. At least that's the way the Kings love us. And that's the way I love you too."

Daniel hung his head in silence at the girl's words. He could barely stand to hear them. Deep inside, he found them hard to believe.

"How can you love without looking at a person's bad points?" Daniel asked. "How can anyone do that?"

"Well, I guess I'm learning how by just doing it," Susan said slowly. "We're in the Kingdom of the Kings. And the greatest gift in their Kingdom is love. That's what the Kingson gives us. And because that love is given to me, I can share it with you. That's why we were sent here. Can you feel it? Can't you sense it? We're in his presence right now."

"We are?" Daniel asked.

"Where do you think all the light is coming from?" John Kramar asked with a friendly smile. "We were told to turn on the lights of our Spirit Flyers. We also knew to use the generators this time because it took more power. Anyway, this is what happened."

Daniel looked at the old red bicycles and noticed that the headlights were turned on. Yet there was light shining in splendor all around. He then looked up at the cloud of glory over his head. The boy blinked in surprise at what he saw in the light. The first time he had seen the face of the Prince of Kings was the day he had been riding with Dirk and his family. That was the day the lock of the chain had been broken. But the Kingson had seemed so mysterious and even distant then. Then he had seen him for that brief moment on the platform.

But this time a quiet awe filled the boy's heart. All the while he had been talking he had not realized the royal presence among them. At first Daniel thought he was afraid, but then he knew that for the first time in a long time he felt good inside. It was the same kind of good feeling you felt when you were high above the clouds on your Spirit Flyer, racing towards the future, knowing something good and exciting was about to happen.

Then the ghostslave shrieked in hideous laughter. "You aren't going anywhere soon, Mr. Rank Blank," the ghostslave said. He held up the ends of a dark chain. At once Daniel's hopes dropped back down.

"But what do I do?" Daniel asked fearfully, looking at the image of himself. "Maybe he's right. Maybe I have reached zero."

"No! You fight!" John Kramar said. "You aren't a slave anymore. The locks of the chain have been broken."

"Then what do I do?" Daniel asked.

"You've got to believe what's true about yourself," John said. "The lies of the ghostslave will bury you, like they almost did. And the only way you break lies is to answer them with truth. Because the Kingson set you free, you have to say it to remind yourself. Say, 'I am free because of the Kingson.' "

"I am free because of the Kingson," Daniel whispered halfheartedly. But when he did, the Big Board shuddered. The message that had been hanging in the darkness still blinked on and off, but it had instantly gotten smaller.

"Say it again," John Kramar said. "The Big Board will tell you lies, so you have to answer it with the truth. That's the fight. Say, 'I belong to the Kingdom of the Kings and I'm free.' "

"I belong to the Kingdom of the Kings," Daniel said with more courage. "I am free."

The Big Board paused at the words. The flashing message suddenly shrunk down to letters only a few inches high. And inside the darkness, the ghostslave image screamed out as if he had been touched by fire, "Noooooooooooo!"

"Tell it the truth about yourself," Susan said, looking from Daniel to the reflection in the Big Board. "Tell it what you read in *The Book of the Kings."*

The words Daniel had read in the old book came into his mind. "I *am* free," Daniel said in a loud voice. "I am a new creation. The old things have passed away. The new has come. The old things have passed away and that means you!" Daniel pointed straight at the distorted reflection of himself.

The ghostslave screamed out in agony, "I hate you. You're a no-good, Rank Blank fool. You're a zero. You have no points. You're pointless. You're a pointless fool in a pointless town in a pointless world, reduced to zero below zero . . . no kings, no nothing . . . and you are a part of that pointless zero nothing . . ."

But Daniel was no longer listening to the lying accusations of the ghostslave. He was remembering all the words he had read in the book, words that had often seemed full of mystery and wonder. "I'm a citizen of the Kingdom," Daniel said louder. "I'm a child of the Kings. I can do all things through him that strengthens me."

"Say it," Susan said with a smile, nodding her head up and down.

"I'm not a slave. I'm free in the Kingdom!" Daniel shouted out. And when he said that, the gobs of slimy darkness fell off the boy and disappeared. At the same time, the reflected ghostslave on the Big Board shrieked and fell backward, the chain fell out of its hands and loosened off Daniel himself and was gone.

Susan and John Kramar both clapped their hands together when they saw the power of the chain broken. Daniel looked down at himself almost in surprise at his boldness. That's when he saw deep inside himself the royal Kingdom light burning in splendor and brightness.

"It was for freedom that the Kingson set me free," Daniel said with a smile. "And I am more than a conqueror in him. Nothing will separate me from the love of the Kings: not points or failures, not death or life, not ghostslaves or chains or powers. There's nothing that can take away their love!"

And with that, Daniel reached in his pocket and pulled out his black shiny number card. He held it up and looked at his face in the dark reflection. Even from the face of the card the ghostslave tried to speak. "The Point System is the only game in town and the only game in the . . ."

But Daniel cocked his arm and threw the flimsy card straight at the Big Board. The card hit with the sound of a crack of thunder. A great sputter of lights and electricity sizzled as the Big Board seemed to go berserk. In an instant, the dark power of the Big Board was split in a roar in the Deeper World.

Daniel felt a rushing tingle all up and down his body as the decision was completed. For an instant, he saw the Prince of Kings himself right in front of him. The Kingson was touching Daniel's right leg with his hand. "I'm granting you your deep wish," the Kingson seemed to whisper. A new sensation shot through Daniel's body.

The great cloud of glorious light lifted away as the Big Board sputtered and smoked and tottered back and forth. "Let's get out of here," Susan yelled. Daniel nodded. He hopped on the back of her bike.

Just as the two red bicycles started to move, the boys lying on the ground began to struggle to their feet, as if coming awake. The boys looked confused, trying to figure out what had happened. That's when they saw the tottering Big Board. "It's going to fall," Barry shrieked.

The boys scrambled and dragged themselves away as fast as they could. The Big Board rocked back and forth. Lights flashed across the surface of the dark panel, spewing out a garble of nonsense letters and numbers. Nothing added up.

But Daniel was hardly paying attention. He was reaching down and feeling his shorter right leg. His leg was still tingling where the Kingson had touched it. In fact, that whole side of his body seemed to be glowing in a new but pleasing sensation. "Something's happening to my leg," Daniel said to Susan over her shoulder. "The Kingson touched it and now something is happening."

Susan aimed the handlebars toward the sky and began pedaling. They hadn't gone ten feet into the air when the Big Board let out a tremendous groan, then fell straight forward. A great screaming sizzle split the air. A haze of dust and smoke rose around the edges of the dark panel as it lay on the field.

Susan was smiling as she pedaled higher into the sky. Daniel looked down at the mess on the ground. People seemed to be running in confused circles like ants. The darkness inside the Big Board looked pale and weak, like the wisps of a broken cobweb. For a moment, the interior of the dark panel seemed to be full of writhing, dying creatures that resembled spiders and insects and snakes. The Big Board sputtered and flashed once more and then went completely and utterly blank.

MRS.
HAPPY'S
COMPLAINT
• • • • • • • •

22

Three days later, the Centerville school opened for the fall. The long summer was finally over. But everyone was still talking about the cheating and the scandal at the awards ceremony. No one knew for sure why the Big Board had fallen the way it had. Most of the parents were blaming the boys on the Rockets. Barry and the other boys were in turn blaming Daniel Bayley and Susan and John Kramar. But when they told what they had seen, none of the adults really believed them. Since the field was partly dark and there was a lot of confusion, the adults gave up trying to determine how the Big Board had fallen.

But the fact remained that the Big Board was down and had stayed down. Though it was a different unit, the Big Board in Happy Toy Store had stopped working at the precise time the other Big Board had fallen.

Happy Toy Store had been a busy place the day school opened. Workmen from Goliath Industries had been running tests all day on the Big Board. That afternoon, a long black limousine pulled up in front of the toy store. Mr. Cyrus Cutright got out of the car. He opened the front door of the store and walked in. Mrs. Happy looked fearfully over at him and then back at the Big Board.

"Big Board, Big Board, on the wall," she said, "who's got the most points of all?" The Big Board glowed while numbers and letters flashed, but when they stopped, it was all gibberish.

"I don't know what to do with it," Mrs. Happy fumed. "It should be working. The mechanical parts seem functional. I've had all sorts of children coming by today, trying to get their new scores. After the Bayley boy disaster, everyone's convinced they've gotten a better rank. They're all begging to see where they are in the Big Picture. I thought some of the little beasts would rip each other apart. I tell you, we're missing a feast of ashes on this as long as the Big Board is down."

The workmen left the store as Mr. Cutright walked over to the Big Board. The wrinkled old man stared at the Board and then at Mrs. Happy. "It's not just this Board either," the old man said with a dry voice. "The Big Board down at the factory was down all day too. I don't like it. I spoke to Mrs. Bayley about the incident. She denied everything, of course. She's not to blame. But I'm beginning to wonder about her. She had to leave work in the middle of the day to take that spoiling snitch of a son of hers to the doctor."

"I hope the little Rank Blank is sick and dies by suppertime for what he did," Mrs. Happy said. "I can't wait to get my hooks in him again. I've already tried, but there's an incredible cloud around him. I can't believe it. The enemy's protecting him just like those Kramar brats."

"Well, he didn't go to the doctor because he was sick," Mr. Cutright said and coughed. "His mother wanted to have some tests to see if he was well."

"Well?" Mrs. Happy said. "What did she mean?"

"She didn't want to talk about it," the old man replied. "But I don't like the looks of it. Usually she's such a cooperative woman. I plan to inquire tomorrow. In the meantime, we've got to get the Big Boards and the Point System rolling again. We're at a critical time and we can't lose momentum. Mr. Smedlowe has agreed to let us install one in the school, and several of the town council members seem agreeable to letting us set them up in town, at the courthouse and the sheriff's office, for starters."

"What about Sheriff Kramar?" Mrs. Happy asked.

"He'll either see the future and be a part of it, or we'll take care of him," Mr. Cutright sneered. "The important thing is not to lose the momentum we've gained. This downtime is going to look bad on your record."

"My record?" the old woman squawked. "You can't blame me for all this."

"Of course I can," Mr. Cutright replied. "The reports have already been sent. Headquarters is aware of your failure. In fact, I thought they may have contacted you by now."

"But that's not fair!" Mrs. Happy said.

"Tut, tut, you know you shouldn't complain," the old man said with a thin smile. "You've fouled up at one of the worst times. We need these Big Boards in place and working. I've heard from the Super Bureau last night that we're getting close to the biggest campaign ever waged in almost two thousand years. By Halloween there's going to be a big push. All ORDER companies like Goliath Industries have to be ready for the shift of power that will come afterward. So when the Boss heard we were having trouble with the Big Boards, I thought the phone would melt right in my hand. You were already on probation for messing up the Toy Campaign."

"Well, I don't intend to have my career ruined by a few Rankety Blank children," Mrs. Happy said angrily. She turned to the Big Board and roared out a string of curses that were so loud they rattled the front windows of the toy store. The Big Board sputtered feebly, then hummed, producing another display of nonsense and gibberish.

"At least the number cards are still out there," Mr. Cutright said. "No one has ever been able to challenge the Point System successfully for long. Even with a few pockets of resistance, they can't turn back the tide of history. They'll live by points or die by points. Just like you."

"But I told you it's not my fault," Mrs. Happy shrieked.

Mr. Cutright smiled again to see the old woman so agitated. "Well, the Big Board giveth, and the Big Board taketh away," he replied. And with that said, the old thin man walked to the front door. He looked once more at the Big Board, walked outside and got in the waiting limousine.

Mrs. Happy stood by the door, watching the car drive off. Then she walked back to try the Big Board again. "The sniveling brats," the old woman muttered as she glared up at the mute panel of darkness. "I hope they choke on their love and forgiveness. But I'll not forget. I'm keeping score and I'll settle it too when I get my chance. I'm counting it all up, and they'll regret the day they crossed me. Headquarters has to understand the problems I've been facing in this miserable little town."

She looked all around the store fearfully, as if someone was sneaking up behind her. And then it happened. In the static and gibberish on the Big Board, a white circle slowly began to form. Inside the circle was a white X. Mrs. Happy stared in horror as the white circle grew larger and larger.

"No," she said. "It's not my fault. This isn't fair. I want to make a Formal Protest to Headquarters that I did all I was supposed to from—"

As she spoke, the circle opened. There was only a short hissing sound as Mrs. Happy was instantly sucked through into the darkness. Then no one was in the toy store. The circled X disappeared. Once again, the Big Board filled up with a gibberish display of letters and numbers which flashed on and off in a static hum.

ROYAL
RIDERS
· · · · · · · · ·
23

Daniel Bayley raced his Spirit Flyer down Tenth Street, heading for the square. He was so happy he didn't even notice the slow-moving black limousine that passed him in the opposite direction.

When he got to the square he slowed the old red bike down. Then he shot across the street to the sidewalk on the inside of the square. Susan and John Kramar were sitting on their Spirit Flyers by the old wooden bandstand, waiting for Daniel.

"We were worried when you weren't in school today," Susan said. "I thought something awful might have happened."

"Something great has happened," Daniel said with a grin. He parked his bike and knocked down the kickstand. "Look at this." The red-headed boy walked in a circle and then jumped up and down.

"Your leg! It looks better," John Kramar said with surprise.

"Not only looks better, it is better," Daniel said, almost bursting. "I thought it was better the night the Big Board fell, but I really wasn't sure. I thought the Kingson said he was granting me my wish. I figured it was just all the excitement of the awards ceremony and so forth. Then on Sunday and Monday it just felt better and better. I told my mother, but she didn't believe me. But when I woke up this morning, it felt great. I didn't even notice that I was walking right until I got downstairs."

"What did your mother say?" Susan asked.

"She didn't know what to say," Daniel replied. "I told her about how I had seen the Kingson. I told her that you can ask him for things and a lot of times he'll do what you wish. She started to get mad, but then I asked her how else I could be walking. She thought I was faking it for a while. But she alters all my pants and the pant leg on my right leg was exactly two inches too short. So then she decided to take me to the doctor. That's why I didn't go to school. She wanted to check it out. She didn't really say it, but she thought I was still faking it somehow. She couldn't believe it."

"What did the doctor say?" John asked.

"Well, Dr. Brimberry has my medical records from my old doctor," Daniel replied. "And they have the last x-rays which were made a few weeks before we moved here. He took some more x-rays and compared them."

"Well?" Susan asked with a smile. "Don't keep us in suspense."

"The x-rays show the bone in my right leg is almost identical in length to my left leg," Daniel said. "Dr. Brimberry says that he's never seen anything like it. He didn't think it was possible. He even asked my mom if those were the real x-rays. He said he could see the remains of an injured place about an inch and a half from the bottom of the bone, but that everything looks normal."

"What did your mom say to that?" John asked.

"Nothing," Daniel said. He got quiet. For a moment the joy seemed to leave his face. "I told her in the car on the way home about what happened that night all over again. She didn't say anything. She just looked real tired."

"She didn't say anything?" Susan asked.

"Not really," Daniel said. "She usually has a lot to say about any little thing, but not this. I think she's still stunned. I told her that I could give her a ride on my Spirit Flyer if she wanted."

"That would be great," John said. "Only sometimes, if they don't believe they can fly, something happens and the bikes don't work as well. I tried to get Roger Darrow to go on a ride once, but he thought it was so strange it didn't really work right. I still don't know what happened."

"That's the hard thing about riding Spirit Flyers," Susan said. "You think you know how they work, then they surprise you. And the Kingson even surprises you more. In *The Book of the Kings* there's lots of stories about him making sick people well. I didn't know he would still do that."

"Well, they say he's the same yesterday and today and forever," Daniel said. "Maybe he still does all sorts of stuff. Stuff we can't even imagine."

The children were all quiet for a moment. Daniel got back on his Spirit Flyer and began pedaling. Susan and John followed. They rode together without speaking through the quiet streets of Centerville. Daniel was the one who led them out to Cemetery Road.

The Goliath Industries factory seemed bigger and darker than ever as they rode west out of town. Smoke was puffing into the air out of the top of the two tall smokestacks. Daniel braked his bicycle to a halt when they reached the beginning of the fence that surrounded the factory. The children looked at the old buildings in silence.

"My mom said the Big Board wasn't working in the factory this morning and that Mr. Cutright was asking her about it," Daniel said softly.

"That could mean trouble," Susan said. "Maybe not this week or the next, but someday."

"That's what I think," Daniel replied. "I think that's maybe why my mom was so quiet. She knows there'll be trouble if she really gets to know the Kings. Goliath Industries runs on the Point System."

"My dad says the city council is planning to buy Big Boards for the town too," Susan said. "But I don't think we should be afraid."

"My number card came back," Daniel said. "It was on my dresser this morning."

"They always come back," John Kramar said. "I just try to ignore it."

"That's right," Susan said. "The Point System will probably always be around in one form or another. I think we are meant to do the best we can with the gifts we've got. The Kings want us to be responsible. But we don't have to be a slave to a bunch of stupid points. Either people accept you for what you are or they don't."

"The hard part is not counting it against them when they call you names," Daniel said. "I don't know if I'll ever be able to look at people without seeing their bad points."

"But that's what the gift of love is all about," Susan said. "And since it's a gift from the Kings, you just sort of use it when you need to."

"Which is about all of the time," John said. "I know I get mad too easily."

"They may call us names and things, but let them," Susan said. "We won't melt. We belong in the Kingdom of the Kings. We don't have to play by the rules of the Point System either. It isn't the only game in town. Royal love is more powerful than anything because it comes straight from the hearts of the Kings."

"And if one of us starts getting dragged back in the Point System, we can help each other, right?" Daniel asked. A new look of hope crossed the boy's face.

"That's right," Susan said. She patted Daniel on the back. "That's what love is all about, watching out for your friends. I think rough times may be coming. *The Book of the Kings* talks about a time when things will really get tough for all those who belong in the Kingdom of the Three Kings."

"I read about that," Daniel said. "But I think it's going to be worse for those who don't know or believe in the Kings."

"Maybe," Susan said. The children all were quiet. They looked at the dark smoke drifting up into the sky above the factory. A breeze was blowing the smoke toward Centerville.

"But we don't need to worry," Susan said. "You're riding your Spirit Flyer again, and the Big Board isn't working. All the kids were talking about it today in school. If the Kings can do it once, they can do it again. We just have to stick together."

"That's right," Daniel said. "I think there's going to be a lot of work to do in the future. And if they want to play rough, we'll just have to be ready. Like the Kingson says, we are more than conquerors because of him."

And with those words, the children cheered and began pedaling rapidly down the road. As they passed the other end of the chain-link fence surrounding the factory, Daniel aimed his handlebars toward the sky. As the old red bicycle rose into the air, he was flanked on both sides by Susan and John.

"We are free," Daniel said to the others as they skimmed over the tops of the trees. "We are in the family of the Kings."

"New creations!" Susan shouted.

"Made for freedom!" John added at the top of his lungs. They all laughed.

And with that said, the royal riders stood up on the pedals of the Spirit Flyers and raced toward the clouds above. Side by side they rose higher and higher to the upward calling of freedom, because it was for freedom that these riders had been set free.

*John Bibee, author of
The Spirit Flyer Series,
lives in Austin, Texas, with
his wife and two children.*